Walking with Angels

Walking with Angels

Lanaya A. Pickett

iUniverse, Inc.
Bloomington

Walking with Angels

This is a work of fiction. All of the characters, names, incidents, organizations, and dialogue in this novel are either the products of the author's imagination or are used fictitiously.

iUniverse books may be ordered through booksellers or by contacting:

iUniverse
1663 Liberty Drive
Bloomington, IN 47403
www.iuniverse.com
1-800-Authors (1-800-288-4677)

Because of the dynamic nature of the Internet, any web addresses or links contained in this book may have changed since publication and may no longer be valid. The views expressed in this work are solely those of the author and do not necessarily reflect the views of the publisher, and the publisher hereby disclaims any responsibility for them.

Any people depicted in stock imagery provided by Thinkstock are models, and such images are being used for illustrative purposes only.
Certain stock imagery © Thinkstock.

ISBN: 978-1-4620-2307-3 (pbk)
ISBN: 978-1-4620-2306-6 (clth)
ISBN: 978-1-4620-2308-0 (ebk)

Library of Congress Control Number: 2011909302

Printed in the United States of America

iUniverse rev. date: 06/01/2011

Chapter 1

I was running for what seemed like forever, running away from the people who called that place an orphanage. I wasn't going to stop. I wasn't going to turn myself back in again. I was really done with that place.

I heard the chants of my fellow orphans yelling behind me.

"Keep running!"

"Don't look back!"

"You deserve to be free!"

Then I heard the screaming from the people who were coming after me.

"Where are you gonna go?"

"Get back here you worthless rat!"

"Zoey get back here now!"

But I wasn't stopping. This was the third time I had run away. The first time I had gotten caught by the police. The second time I came back because I didn't have a place to turn to. But this time I wasn't going back. Three times is the charm, right? I had been beaten, hurt and raped too much to stay in that place.

I ran into a park and hid beneath big bushes. I heard the steps in front of me getting closer so I put my hand over my mouth to stop my heavy breathing.

"Zoey Where are you?" It felt funny to hear my middle name coming from these people. I was sent here when I was about three years old. My mother couldn't take care of me so she left me there. She said she would come back for me but that was fourteen years ago and I knew my life wouldn't be the same. The name I was truly given was Roel Zoey Somers. But the orphanage wanted to change it.

"Come out come out where ever you are," said the other owner of the orphanage.

"Jack," said the other guy. I didn't really get to know their names so I didn't know who was who. "It's getting too dark and a storm is coming. We'll never be able to find a dirty girl in the rain. Maybe we should look for her in the morning."

Jack was quiet for what seemed like forever and I thought I was caught. He looked to the sky and sure enough dark menacing clouds began to form. "Fine but we start in the park. If we don't find her by tomorrow we're going to the police," he said and walked out of the park.

I sat for a while waiting for the right time to check and see if someone found me. I looked up and noticed I was alone. I walked to the other end of the park and found a place to lie down under a tree.

Just my luck it started to rain hard and cold. I went into my backpack and got out my blanket and set it down where I laid.

I was just about sleep when I felt someone put a jacket over me and pick me up. I unwillingly put my head on their shoulder while they started walking. I didn't know who it was but they were incredibly warm and cozy. I knew I want in the arms of someone like Jack.

My initial actions were to kick and scream but something in me knew I was safe. I have problems trusting people so this shouldn't be so comforting. But as I thought more about it the more I felt safe. I simply told myself I'll fight with this soft stranger another time.

I woke up in a room as bright as the sun. It was completely yellow and orange and very bright. The covers on the bed were a lemon yellow and much too bright for my eyes to bear.

"Rise and shine sleepy head," someone yelled making me fall out of the bed screaming.

"Ahh, who the hell are you and where am I," I yelled back trying to focus my eyes on him. I must've had a good sleep.

He laughed lightly and said, "My name is Chad and this is my room. And this is my house." He was very cute. He had long brown hair with dark grey eyes. He was tall and beautifully pale. He was muscular yet very lean. He was the hot bad boy minus the yellow room and A.D.D.-tweeker-type personality.

I tried to remember how I got here but my brain seemed fried and still asleep. "How-how'd I get here?"

"I brought you here, duh," he said as if I should know that. "I didn't want to leave you in the rain because you are way too pretty to be outside in the cold and rain."

"Besides that why did you bring me here," I asked a bit confused. "You could've brought me to the police station or the orphanage," even though I knew I didn't want to go back there.

"I don't think you want to back there," he laughed. "You were running from there so why would you go back?"

He's got a point. "Um, how'd you know I was running from there," I asked.

"Do you really want to go back to the orphanage?" He asked knowingly.

"Do you live alone," I asked picking up what I hoped was a brown shirt.

"I have four other siblings. They're all boys by the way." He said as if it was something simple.

My eyes went so wide as though they would pop out of my face. "All boys," I yelled at the top of my lungs. "I'm not living with all boys."

"You don't have to count me as a boy you live with," he said with a confident smile. "I'm gay."

"Like I didn't know that," I laughed. He's sitting in an orange and yellow room. Why wouldn't he be gay? "No prejudice here," I added.

"That's another place where you come in." He smiled a wide mischievous smile. "I need a girl to go shopping with me."

I looked down at my clothes and laughed nervously. "Um, if you haven't noticed I didn't fall from a fashion school."

"I see that," he said and looked at my clothes. He took my hand and led me to his bathroom which was quite big. "Here," he said handing me a towel and a rag. "Take a shower and I'll give you some clothes. I might have some girl clothes in my mom's old room that you can wear." He said and walked out of the bathroom.

Getting in that shower felt like heaven. The water was steaming hot and the pressure was just right. For about ten minutes I let the water run on my body and hair before I mustered up the strength to finally wash up and get out. I put the towel around and walked past the long mirror in the bathroom.

I jumped at the girl that used to be me before I was neglected a shower. My hair color was finally noticeable. It was some type of black with hints of purple and blue. It was like looking at the night sky just after the moon went down and before the sun came up. Yet it fit my copper pale complexion perfectly and my deep sea blue eyes. My eyes weren't a normal color. I was gracefully short and skinny, not sick skinny but

4

fit skinny. My skin wasn't like a regular color. It was a type of tanned pale color. Yet everything about me blended in with each other.

I walked back into Chad's room and found a note and some jeans and a long sleeved shirt on the bed.

Hey I went downstairs to talk to my brothers. They are probably choking the hell out of me by now so please come to my rescue.

Chad.

I got dressed in lightning speed and hurried out the door. His door was at the end of the hall so I turned right towards what I thought was the stairs.

His room was completely different from the house. The walls were dark red with gold trimmings and designs. It had an ancient feeling to it but it was beautiful.

I heard what seemed to be yelling coming from another hallway so I turned and slid down the very hard stairs and landed butt-first in the kitchen. With my uncanny balance and late as ever reflexes I'll be dead my sundown.

Chad was at my side in seconds laughing his ass off. "Goodness, are you okay?"

I was giggling like a school girl and trying to talk at the same time. "I'm fine," I said sighing as he helped me up. My smile faded when I saw three other gorgeous men standing in the kitchen.

"This is her," one of them asked. His deep voice made shivers shake my whole body. He didn't sound mad. It was more an amused authority figure-type voice.

"Yes, guys I want you to meet our new maid," then he went quiet.

I looked up and noticed him struggling to find a name. "Zoey, my name is Zoey," I said. "And I'm not going to be anyone's maid." I looked around in disgust at the floor that needed mopping and the sky-high pile of dishes in the sink. "But you are in desperate need of one." He looked at me and smiled.

"Not what I was going for but it'll do for now," Chad said almost smirking. Then he continued, "Let's not be rude, boys."

The one who spoke earlier walked over to me and smiled, "My name is Dean. I'm the oldest in the house." He was far beyond gorgeous. He had long black hair that was pulled back into a ponytail. His eyes were a bright green that made you think of plants. He was muscular but didn't look too beefy. He was the type that worked out but not too much. He was tall and tanned. He was hot.

"Anyway," one of the others said. "My name is Jared. If you need a laugh I'm your guy." He was kind of cute in a goofy way. He had dirty blood hair and pretty blue eyes. He wasn't as tall as Chad and Dean but he was tall. His skin was pale white but it fit him perfectly. "And this one her is Eric. He's very shy."

Eric was small. He was just a few inches above me. He had spiked black hair with the prettiest light grey eyes. His skin was not as pale as Jared's but he was gorgeous. "Hi," he said in the smallest voice I'd ever heard.

"Hello," I said to all of them. Chad had told me that there were four other guys besides him that lived here.

But before I could utter the question the kitchen door swung open and the most gorgeous creature walked in. He instantly took my breath away. He had honey brown hair with light streaks of blonde. He was tall and lean but under his tight shirt you could tell he had many muscles. His skin wasn't as pale as Eric yet it wasn't as tanned as Dean. He almost looked like he was orange.

The most intriguing things about him were his eyes. They were orange. They were so beautiful behind his hair. His eyes were so intense it made me think of a forest fire whipping through the trees turning the sky black with clouds and orange with angry fire. They were just so mad.

"Who is she?" he yelled at Chad. "And why the hell did you bring her here?"

"She needs a place to stay," he looked toward the kitchen that was in need for a good cleaning, "and we need a maid."

"Like we need a maid," he said coming to stand in front of me. "Who the hell are you?"

Ouch. Who the hell is he to hurt my feelings? "My," this asshole wasn't going to intimidate me. I stood with my barely there chest high and glared at him. "My name is Zoey."

"Well Zoey, I think it'll be best if you leave." His breath was like tangy oranges and sweet tangerines.

I looked down and then to Chad who had pleading eyes. "But I have nowhere else to go."

The mysterious boy looked furious. "Don't you have parents? Can't you live with them?"

I laughed at the thought of having my mom with me right now. "My mom left me at an orphanage when I was three."

"So why don't I take you back there," he said grabbing my hand. When he touched me he sent sparks through my body.

I snatched my hand away from his and backed up to the stairs. "I'm not going back there." He irritates me.

"And why not," he said matching my anger.

I felt a soft wind brush over my arms and lift the sleeve of my shirt. When it did it revealed the black, purple and blue marks running up and down my arm.

7

That made them all stop and stare. Yeah, this isn't embarrassing at all.

Chad slowly walked up to me with his mouth fixing to find words. "Wha—how—who did this," he said so quietly I almost didn't hear him.

I quickly pulled my sleeve over my arm and stepped away. "The people at the orphanage did it. They don't do it to all the kids. I haven't been their favorite with all the trouble I gave them."

"Julian if you take her back there I'll never talk to you again," Chad said in the most serious voice.

Julian smiled wickedly, "Is that a promise?"

Anger and rage burned through Chad's eyes before he looked at Julian. "I'm serious, they're hurting her, Julian," he yelled at the top of his lungs. "If you have some type of heart you would let her stay." He said lower this time.

A burst of loud and annoying arguing erupted between Dean, Julian and Chad. Jared looked like he was trying to figure out if he should make a joke out of this or not. Eric was slowly walking up the stairs. He seems like he just doesn't want to be a part of the situation.

"Hey guys can you stop yelling please?" I asked but no one heard me. "Hey, are you gonna listen to the point of the problem? Would you shut up for a minute?" So I did what any teenage girl would do, scream at the top of their lungs.

They all turned to me with shocked faces. I was too upset to think about how mad they looked. "So here's the thing, I'm not happy about this little staying-with-five-boys-thing. But I'm not going to live out on the freaking street like I did before. I sure as hell don't like the fact that I was nominated maid. But if it keeps me here then fine I'm here. So besides Mr. Hot and Grumpy, does anybody else want me out? Majority wins?" I leaned against the wall and glared at the fuming orange flame spewing hot fumes with his eyes.

Five minutes went by and nobody objected or voted me off the island, figuratively speaking, so I started cleaning. Finally they parted ways until Julian was the only one left.

He was staring aimlessly in the fridge, in the kitchen; therefore he was in my way. "It would be nice if you could get out of my way while I'm cleaning."

He sighed angrily and spun to face me. "It would be nice if you would just get out of my way," he said and stalked upstairs.

I smiled secretly to myself, "but you got out of my way," I said when I knew he was not in earshot of me.

It was silent for a moment and I went to get me something to eat. I made a ham sandwich and sat back down.

"So Zoey," he started and I stopped him.

"My name isn't Zoey," I said. "I wanted you guys to think my name was Zoey."

He was very silent for a while before chuckling once. "What is it?"

"Roel," I said. "I'm not a big fan of it because-"

"It's a boy's name," he finished with a disgusted tone. "I see why you don't like it. Doesn't it mean rock or something?"

"Are you making fun of me," I asked glaring at him.

"No," he said with contained laughter. "I just think it's horrible that you have a boy's name."

Did he really just say that? I gave him a look that silently conveyed that he's a serious asshole.

I stormed back to my room and slammed the door hard. I tried to get my mind off of the way Julian treated me. *Why should I even care,* I thought, *he's a jerk.* He was a jerk that didn't have to treat me like I did something wrong.

I went to open the door that I thought was the closet but found a bathroom. It was big and beautiful. The walls were white and the shower and floor were as blue as my room. The mirror had exquisite gold and silver framing around it.

I went back into my room and went to get some underwear and a towel. I went to take a shower for the second time today. The water was the better than Chad's shower. I felt so much more relaxed and less angry than I was.

When I got out of the shower I washed my face and went back into my room. Dean was sitting on my bed.

"Is this going to be a pedophile-I'm depressed and I want to watch an underage girl sleep while I think of ways to kills her—kind of thing because if it is then I'll leave." I said covering my exposed body.

He blushed a little and said," Don't worry I'm not here to spy on you. I wanted to know if you were thinking of getting paid for cleaning the house."

"I don't know," I said thoughtfully. "Well, it would be nice to get paid for a job I didn't apply for."

"Fine you can do that," he said and got up and walked to the door. "You are very good at what you do so I wouldn't be upset if you stayed with us for a long while."

I smiled to myself and lay down on my bed. I felt accomplished and calm until an angry knock on the door disturbed.

"What do you want?" I asked through the pillow.

"Can I come in," the voice said booming through my door. Julian didn't really wait for my answer and I still wonder why he even asked.

"Yea, Julian it's all right you can come in. I'm not half naked or anything," I said sarcastically then threw on an overly sized t-shirt that appeared out of nowhere.

"Why did you walk away," he asked in a confused voice.

"I wanted to get away from the ass-jerk named Julian," I said simply and smart-aleck ass, "duh."

He looked at me with a little amusement. "Very cute, Roel," he said sarcastically. "But why did you get mad?"

"I've been talked about enough by kids and so-called adults at the orphanage because of my name," I said turning my head to look at him. His eyes confirmed that he understood.

His eyes were so deep and angry it made me feel like a child. He always made my heart jump when he made eye contact. And when he said my name I felt like I could melt under his control.

He looked at me with thought and curiosity. "Why didn't you tell us when we came here?"

"I really don't like my first name," I said looking at my bed and fiddling with my hair. "Plus I was talked about my entire life for having a boy's name."

"Well I think that the name suits you," he said pushing my hair out of my face.

I looked up at him and smiled, "Thanks."

His eyes were soft for the first time and you could see the vulnerability in them. There was a sadness that they held that made him look so innocent. But that was gone just as fast as it came.

"No problem," he said bringing back his anger and closeness. He stood up and started for the door. "You should get some sleep. You had a long day," he said and walked out the door.

I lie on the bed and fell fast asleep. I started to dream. It started as any dream with lights and colors. In the dream I opened my eyes to a beautiful meadow and a clear water lake. It was a clear blue sky that softly licked the lake at the end of the horizon.

I turned to my left and the dream turned into a nightmare. My house was on fire and my mom was still in the house. Flashbacks of when our house burned down came like lightning and I jolted upright out of the dream.

I had sweat all over me and I was breathing heavy. I looked around my room and found it was still night. I got up from my bed, put some slippers on and stepped out of my room.

For the most part I was sick of running into Julian in the hallway. "Oh, gosh what are you doing up," I asked scared half to death.

"If you would just go to sleep then you wouldn't need to why I'm up." He said rudely.

I was just about done with his attitude, "What did I do to you?"

He walked down stairs and I walked behind him, "You came here," he said turning to face me. "And don't follow me."

"I won't," I said wanting to shove my fist down his throat. "Listen," I said calmer, "I don't want to be the bearer of bad news but I'm not going anywhere for a while. You really need to get over yourself and take a good look in the mirror and check your attitude. I think you should get used to seeing my face because it'll be right there all the time." I said and walked back upstairs.

That night Julian didn't go on his little walk because he sat by my door almost the whole night. He didn't know I knew but he wasn't that hard to hear. He kept mumbling things about me while walking back and forth in front of my door. But yet I felt protected and safe. Soon enough I fell asleep but not until I heard him whisper, "Roel I'm sorry," and walk away.

Chapter 3

I woke up to the blinding sun in my eyes. I didn't quite remember what happened yesterday due to the fact that I thought it was all a dream. I thought I would be back in my cot at the orphanage and looking at the hopeless faces of the young boys and girls who were in the same predicament I was in.

But no, I woke up to the ocean blue walls and white carpet of the room I thought I dreamed up. I smiled and reminded myself that I was out of that place for good. I got up from my comfortable bed and stretched long and hard. I didn't have a sore bone in my body and I was feeling extra refreshed. I heard shuffling on the other side of my door so I went to go see who or what it was.

To my surprise, note the sarcasm, it was Julian pacing back and forth in front of my room. "Dude I'm trying to sleep here. What the hell are you doing?" I asked.

He stopped and turned to me, "You need to see Chad. Something's wrong with him." He grabbed my arm and pulled me to Chad's room. "His door is locked and wants to only see you." He hammered his fist on the door.

"Jeez not so loud," I whisper and knock on the door myself. "Chad, are you okay?" I knocked on the door again and waited for an answer. I hear the bed post screech and footsteps slowly came to the door.

"Ro, is that you," he asked and a terribly broken voice.

"Yes it's me Chad. Can I come in," I asked pushing Julian away from the door. "Go away," I whispered to him.

I heard the door unlock and I walked in. His room was almost just the way I left it except for the bed being disheveled from sleeping in it. He was lying on the floor with a candy apple red face and puffing red eyes. "Hey," I said quietly, "what's wrong?"

"Um," he paused and looked at me, "I'm tired of being gay!" he started crying hysterically and I tried to hold back laughter.

"Um, what," I said through small giggles. "Why are you tired of-?"

"Don't laugh at me," he said getting up from the floor and jumping on the bed. "Do you know hard it is to be in a house full of boys and you know they look at you weird because I'm gay?" He looked like he was waiting for an answer so I just shook my head. "Well I know you wouldn't but I mean they laugh at me when I come home wearing pink and purple. They make fun of how I talk and the way I walk. I hate being gay around them."

We sat in an awkward silence for a moment before I thought of something helpful to say. "Don't let them get to you," I said simply.

He looked at me like that was impossible. "How do I do that?"

"Ignore them," I said. "When I was in the orphanage I was being treated like shit from many people because of how short I was and because I was weird looking. Bright blue eyes and caramel skin doesn't look right." I sat down on the bed and fiddled with my fingers. I haven't really talked about this to anyone. So how do I know I can trust them? "They would say to me that my mom didn't want me at all. I knew they were lying so I didn't let that stop me from being who I am. I was still going to try and find my mom. I just smiled at them and told them that she would come for me one day." I looked at him and saw that I was making him feel a little better. "If the guys are picking on you just tell them they're dicks and turn the other cheek." He started laughing and I saw the Chad I first met. "And if that doesn't work then they'll have to answer to me and my fist of fury," I put my fists up in the boxing position and mimicked a serious combo to the face.

"Thanks Ro," he gave me a hug and I stopped up short for a moment but embraced him back. "You really have good advice."

I grabbed his hand and towed him to the door, "C'mon, let's go get some breakfast."

We walked out his door and ran into Dean. "What is wrong with your gay ass," he asked making Chad tighten his grip on my hand.

"Hey lay off," I say stepping between him and Dean. "He's had a rough morning. Stop being a dick," I said dragging the reluctant Chad along.

Dean turned towards me with shock and amusement on his face. "What did you just call me," he gasped.

I turned to him and stood my ground, "I called you a dick. If you guys keep picking on Chad then I'll have something to do about it." I turned and stopped then turned back. "And every time you call him gay, mention his like for wood or man mean, or refer to him as a homosexual, he and I will call you guys dicks," I turned to Julian and the rest of the siblings that came into the hallway, "all of you." I turned around and grabbed Chad's hand and went downstairs.

"Wow," he said, mouth ajar, "That was incredible. Why did you stick up for me like that?"

18

"That's what friends do, ya know," I said getting out the bacon and eggs to make sandwiches. "Plus, you need a shopping buddy, right?"

He started laughing and jumping up and down, "Hell yea!"

Eric groggily slumped down the stairs with a serious case of bed head. He said good morning but I didn't hear it through the yawn and mumbling.

"Hey Eric," Chad said. "Do you wanna go out with us today? We need to go shopping for miss orphan over here."

"Yea, sure, whatever," was all he said. He grabbed a sunny delight and headed back upstairs.

I cooked bacon and egg sandwiches for everyone. One by one everyone was sitting at some part of the kitchen stuffing their mouths with bacon egg sandwiches.

"God, girl you can cook," Dean said through bites of food. "Where did you learned to cook like this?"

"The first time I cooked at the orphanage it was a bacon and egg sandwiches and I loved cooking ever since," I said smiling to myself. "Ever since I can remember, I've been obsessed with cooking."

"Well you're good at it," Jared said finishing his plate. "And I'm not just talking about your looks."

"Thank you," I said blushing madly. "I didn't think they were that good," I said.

"They're amazing," Eric said quietly sitting next to me. "Is there a recipe for this?"

"Sadly no," I said. "I just make it when I'm thinking about it."

"You need to think about it every morning," Chad said stuffing the rest in his mouth trying to look manlier. I just laughed at him because he looked ridiculous.

I got compliments from everyone except for Julian who just ate his food and went back upstairs. It irked my nerves how rude he was treating me. "What the hell is that about," I asked Chad and Eric who were as stunned as I was.

"I actually don't know," Chad said. "He usually has something to say about someone's cooking whether it is good or bad."

I got a little angry but I let it go just as fast. "Well if he doesn't say something about it then I won't cook for him."

Eric laughed and said, "That'll teach him a lesson."

We laughed about that for a few seconds before he came back down stairs. "Don't cook for me at dinner," he said before walking out the door.

Still in my Pj's, I went out the door behind him. "And where will you be," I asked yelling at him.

"I won't be here," he said simply. "So you have fewer dishes to wash."

That comment stung a bit and I felt a tear escape from my eye. "If you don't eat tonight then don't eat here again," I yelled before slamming the door.

I stood facing the door for about two minute before storming off to take a shower.

The shower felt less comforting due to the fact that I was so angry. It didn't calm and sooth me like I wanted it to. It made me feel worse and I couldn't feel anything but repressed anger.

I got out the shower and went to my bedroom. I got halfway back into the bathroom when I found Eric sitting on my bed. "Why can't you guys make sounds," I yelled at him looking for some of Chad's mom's clothes. I found a pair of sixties looking blue jeans and slid them on. They were unexpectedly warm and comfy. I found a simple white t-shirt and slipped it on with my jeans.

"Sorry to startle you," he said with a sly smile on his face. He turned serious for a second. "Are you okay with what happened with you and Julian," he asked in a low tone.

"I'm fine," I lied. He gave me a "get real" look so I told the truth. "No, I'm not fine with what he did," I said. "He gets under my skin a lot."

"Well if you must know, he is doing this for your sake."

I laughed humorlessly, "And how is being rude to me good for my sake?"

"Just let time run its course." He said getting up and walking to the door. "He'll come around soon enough." He walked out the door and left me alone.

"Thanks Eric," I said under my breath and went out to the hallway. I went to the living room and found everyone sitting around Chad while he played video games.

"What are you guys doing," I asked sitting next to Jared.

"We always watch Chad while he plays video games," Jared said focusing on the game in front of his face. "He's ridiculously good at it."

"Oh," was all I could say due to the fact the Chad was killing just about everything they looked like a monster.

For the next few hours we sat and watched Chad as he put all his anger into the killing of zombies and unknown scary-looking beasts. Julian walked in and sat on the floor next to Chad and Eric.

I couldn't help but feel his eyes staring at me. When I looked over to him he would turn his head and act like he was paying attention to what Chad and Dean were now playing.

Time passed and I fell asleep on Jared's shoulder. I felt so relaxed and calm that I didn't even notice Jared get up and leave. He laid me down softly on the couch making sure I didn't wake up.

I woke up still in the place I fell asleep and found Julian asleep across the room. He looked as peaceful as an angel. His face wasn't stuck in his permanent scowl and his features were strong but soft. He looked so sad while he slept. My heart felt a twinge for how he acted toward everyone. I just hoped that one day this face that I'm seeing can be seen when he was awake.

He must have sensed me looking at him because he started stirring in his sleep. He looked at me before turning over on the floor and going back to sleep. I got to see his angel face when he was awake and it was still peaceful.

I looked out the window and noticed the sun was just beginning to rise. I groggily got up and went to my room to finish my slumber. That night was the first night I dreamt of Julian and it didn't turn into a nightmare.

The dream was peaceful and serene. I was sitting on a beach with a beautiful white mini-dress on. The beach was quite like my room with white sand and multi-color blue sea. There was a small house on the shore and Julian was sitting on the porch. He was wearing a white t-shirt and blue jeans.

"Don't you look beautiful," he said with happiness lighting up his face. He walked toward me and faced the ocean. "Isn't it pretty," he asked looking at me.

I was as dumbfounded as ever at this point. "I hope this is a dream. You with a smile on your face and me in a dress, this can't be real." I said looking very confused.

"I thought you might want to see something new for a change," he said before turning back to the ocean. "Look," he said as he put his head down. "I haven't been the nicest person to you but I can't let you get too close to me."

"What do you mean," I asked wonderingly.

"I mean," he looked me in the eyes and a tear escaped from his eye. "I can't be around you."

"Why," I asked in almost sad tone. "What did I do to you?"

"His face became a sickening sneer, "You came here, Roel! I don't want you here and you're here!" he walked off the beach and into the cabin with no more explanation.

He left me on the beach with tears framing my face. I sunk down to the sand and cried some more. *Why are you crying?* I thought to myself. *You've just met him and you don't need to be around him if he doesn't like. Why do you even care, Roel? He's not worth the pain.*

I woke from my slumber and looked around. I realized with was about 1 or 2:00 in the afternoon and I was alone. Dean left a note for me on the table:

Zoey,

We went to the mall and left you to get some rest. Chad is shopping for you while Jared, Eric and I are handling some things. Don't worry about cleaning the house today, it's clean enough. Julian is home with you so play nice. Make sure you at least cook dinner for us when we get home.

-Dean

So I was home with Julian, great. I really didn't want to deal with him and his attitude but I guess I will have to endure it. I also had to make dinner. I hope they like spaghetti because that's all I'm making.

I made myself a bacon and egg sandwich. I made one for Julian and set it on the island I the kitchen.

I went back into the living thinking I had time to lounge around before I started cooking. I found the remote and turned on the TV. It was nothing really on

TV so I went back into the kitchen. I nearly jump out of my skin when I saw Julian sitting at the island.

He was slumped over in his chair eating the sandwich. Just looking at him brought back the memories of my dream and how peaceful he looked in his sleep. He sure didn't look like that now.

"What are you looking at," he said ruthlessly.

I snapped out of my trance and retorted quickly, "Why do you have to be such a dick with a capital "D"?"

"I was born that way," he shot back.

"Well, I was born with these eyes so they can look where ever they want. Is that a problem?" I shot back with a mocking tone.

"Are you willing to try me," he asked getting up from his seat.

"Depends," I said smirking a little, "What kind of test is it?"

He grabbed my arm and pulled me close to him. "It's a test where you lose, I win and everything goes back to normal."

His grip on my arm was a little painful but I wasn't going to let him see it. "Do your worst tough guy," I said looking him in the eyes trying not to show fear.

"You're nothing but a stupid little girl," he said as he let my arm go. He turned away from me and started walking toward the stairs.

I was so angry with him that I shot a pan at his head. It grazed his ear and hit the wall causing him to jump a little. He stood frozen for a moment before turning to me with literal fire in his eyes.

"You have no idea what I can do to you yet you insist on provoking me," he said walking over to me slowly.

I started to get a little freaked out at how orange his eyes looked. They looked like they were actually flickering with flames and burning holes through me. "You don't scare me, you know that right," I said putting a little bravado in my voice to hide the cracking of my voice.

"Then why do I sense a feeling of being scared all over you," he was almost in my face by this moment. The look on his face told me he was quite angry and fed up with me. "How about this, stay out of my way and I'll spare your life?"

I took that a little too deep and it made me angry, "Is that a threat, Julian? I don't take threats lightly."

"Then I think you should really try to stay away from me." He turned and walked back upstairs.

"Dick," I yelled out as he slammed his door.

"Bite me," he said coming from the other side of the door.

I didn't realize how much his words hurt me until a silent tear rolled down my cheek. I couldn't manage to do anything after that. I left a note for the boys that I would cook when they came home after I decided to retreat to my room and cry a little bit more. I just wished my life wasn't so sad and unbearable.

Hours went by before the others came back and I started cooking. I never came out of my room but heard everyone on the other side of my door talking about me. They were all worried about me and wondered if it was Julian's fault.

I heard a soft knock on the door and knew in an instinct that it was Eric. "Yes Eric," I said.

"Can I come in," he asked his usual calm, quiet voice.

I don't know what it is about these boys and my room but they really don't wait for an answer when coming in my room. "You can come in Eric. Even if I said no you would come in now wouldn't you?"

She got up from the floor with her head facing the door. When she turned to me I swear her eyes were glowing red. "You have no idea what you just got yourself in to," she said before storming out the door.

Both Chad and Julian started yelling at the same time, "Roel what is wrong with you?"

I looked at them confused and startled, "I don't like when people talk to me like that. I'm a person like everyone else and I don't want to be talked down to." I pulled away from them and walked into the kitchen.

Chad walked in on my heels, "Are you nuts? That girl is a vamp-crazy girl. She would do anything to get someone back."

"I don't care what she would do. I don't like being disrespected," I said grabbing pots so I can start cooking.

Julian came into the kitchen and grabbed a pot put of my hand and threw it across the room. "You have to be the stupidest girl I have ever met," he said inches from my face.

I wanted to be scared at that moment but the anger got the best of me. "You think I'll let someone like you or her just stand in front of me and hurt my feelings. I don't care if she was a freaking bat out of hell. I won't stand around and let her say something like that to me and she just get away with it." I looked into his eyes and never turned away. "If you don't like that your girlfriend left then go after her but don't think I'm gonna feel sorry for what I did. I'm not afraid of her or you. I've fought off bigger things than you."

He grabbed me by the neck and lifted me in the air. "You better take that back," he said gripping my neck tighter.

I fought hopelessly and grabbed for his arm. "Julian-you're hurting me," I whispered trying to loosen his grip.

He threw me to the floor and bent down in front. I heard everyone coming downstairs at this point. "You've been warned you silly little nymph," he grabbed my arm and picked me up.

I felt like I was coughing up a lung but it just wouldn't come out. Chad was by my side in an instant and tried to me to my room. I wasn't helping him much because I was still trying to get to Julian. I didn't get close to the stairs when Chad had to pin me to the wall. I didn't know what was wrong with me but I was completely angry and it kept boiling inside of me.

"What the hell is wrong with you," Dean asked Julian.

"She punched Julia in the face," Julian said like it was that simple.

"And I bet Julia said something stupid as hell and Zoey got fed up with her," he said like it happened all the time. "Finally the girl got some sense knocked into her."

Julian reached across the space between him and Dean and hit him across the face, "It was all Roel's fault!"

Dean got up from the floor quick and stood in Julian's face, "Who the hell is Roel?"

"Her," Julian pointed at me and a flash of panic reached my face. But it was gone as fast as it came.

I slipped from Chad's grasp and leaped for Julian. I was cut short by Dean's arm and pinned to the floor. "Let-go-of-me," I spat struggling under Dean's body.

"Zoey, I mean Roel calm down you're burning up," he said trying to sooth me by brushing my hair.

"I don't care," I yelled slipping from under him and reaching for Julian. I grabbed his shirt and punched him in the face. He fell under me and I got on top of him. I started to hit him again but he grabbed my arms.

"Roel stop," he said ever so calm.

I didn't listen and struggled to free my arms.

"Roel I don't want to hurt you," he said getting a little angrier.

I still didn't heed the warning and one of my hands got free. I ripped it across his face leaving scratch marks.

"Roel," he yelled.

I still didn't listen and he grabbed my hand. He flipped my over and I fell on my back. I still didn't stop fighting and he was starting to fume.

He pinned my hand above my head before yelling in my face, "ROEL KNOCK IT OFF!"

That stopped me in my tracks and I looked into his eyes. I saw the angry fire lighting up his eyes and I couldn't help but feel vulnerable. I was breathing heavy and tears started streaming down my face.

"God, what the hell is wrong with you," he said picking me up from the floor. I started to refuse but he put his arms around me and embraced me for a few seconds.

I started pushing his chest and pulling myself back before he could stop me. "Let go of me," I said prying myself away from him and running upstairs.

"Roel wait," Chad called after me. He started running behind me up the stairs.

I shut my door before anyone else but Chad came in my room. "Why did you follow me?"

"I wanted to know if you were okay," he said sitting beside me on my bed. "What happened to you down there? You were s-so angry and wild."

I looked down at my hands and saw Julian's blood on them. "I scratched him hard, didn't I?" I looked at Chad and saw sadness in his eyes. "I was just so angry. He hurt me and so did Julia. I let the anger boil from the first time he ever said something rude to me.

He just makes me so mad," I started getting hot again. I felt like I was on fire and it was increasing.

"Ro you have to calm down," Chad said putting his hands on either side of my face. I closed my eyes and refused to look at anything. "Roel look at me," he said in a serious tone.

I opened my eyes and noticed he was crying. I put my arms around him and pulled him into a hug. "Chad you look so scared," I said crying. "I'm so sorry for scaring you, Chad."

He sniffled a little and pulled away to look at me, "I'm fine. I'm more worried about you and whether you would try to pull that again."

I smiled and looked down, "I'll try not to do that again."

"Good," he said, "Because I don't want to lose you now that I've found you." He seemed have more meaning into that phrase than I thought.

"What do you mean by that," I asked.

"You're like a sister to me and I don't want to lose you," he said looking down.

"You're the one aren't you?"

Chapter 4

"You're the one you told me about earlier," I said looking him in the eye. "You're my brother, aren't you?"

He looked down at the bed and fiddled with his fingers. "Yes I'm your brother but you can't tell anyone. They don't know you're like us . . . ." His voice trailed and he looked into my eyes. It looked like I wasn't supposed to hear that part.

"Like you guys how," I said making him face me.

"You'll find out soon enough Roel. I can't really tell you about certain things." He went to get up from the bed and walk towards the door. "Oh, your new clothes are downstairs waiting for you."

He left me alone in my room again. I went to go wash the blood off my fingernails and take a good look in the mirror.

I didn't see myself anymore. I saw a girl who was being hurt again by people that should care about her. Well she was being hurt by one person that should care about her. I didn't want to be that girl anymore. I wanted to be the one who now had a brother and maybe have a new family.

I smiled to my reflection and went downstairs. I went into the living which was extremely dark for this time of day. I looked out the window and noticed huge clouds filling the sky. I sat in the darkness of the living room thinking about what happened and what I needed to do to make it right.

While I was thinking someone else came into the living room and sat on the floor next to the couch I was sitting on. By the way he let out a frustrating sigh I knew Julian was sitting in here with me.

I didn't know whether I should say something so I just let out a sigh of recognition. He let a little laugh that sounded almost like real laughter.

"I knew you were down here," he said. The sound of his voice made me shake with several emotion; anger, sadness, excitement, passion.

"Well, where else can I actually think without being disturbed," I said trying to be a little humorous. "Everyone just barges into my room."

"This is a good place to think," he said sounding kind of sad.

"Look Julian about today," I started. I wanted to make things right and I was going to start with him. "I wanted to say that I'm s-s-so-so sorry. I mean I'm sorry that I hit you and cut your face. I'm not sorry, however, about hitting your girlfriend."

He laughed full-heartedly and said, "I really didn't expect you to be sorry about anything that happened. I was being a dick for the past few days and it wasn't really your fault."

"Is that an apology Julian," I asked sounding shocked.

"Yea, I think it is an apology, on one condition," he looked up at me.

"Is it bad," I asked a little worried that he might snap at me.

"No," he said getting up from the floor and extending his arm toward me. "Can you fix my face and cut my hair?"

I took his hand as he helped me up. "It'll be my pleasure," I smiled as he led me toward the kitchen. "How bad is your face?"

"Well after you went upstairs Julia came back and put her freshly manicured claws across my face," he flicked on the light and I jumped back at the sight of his face. "Is it that bad?"

"Julian it looks like you got into a fight with a very sharp-clawed cat," I said looking for the first-aid kit. When I found it I sat him down and started to clean up the cuts on his face. The cuts I left looked like paper cuts compared to the deep gashes that were now framing his face. "What did she do, put knives on her fingers and slap you three or four times?"

"Nope, it was just her fingers," he said simply.

I took out the alcohol and he flinched back. "You're more afraid of alcohol than you are of your girlfriends hands?"

"Alcohol stings," he said preparing for the impact of the sting, I guess.

"Well this is going to hurt a little," I said placing an alcohol pad close to his face.

When it touched his skin he screamed in his chest. I made the clean as quick and painless as I could but it didn't help. I felt bad for hurting him so I grabbed his hand. His body tensed when I touched him but he relaxed and took my hand.

"I'm sorry for this," I said quietly. "If I didn't hit your girlfriend she wouldn't have come back and scratched you." When I was putting the bandages on his face he kept his eyes locked on mine and I couldn't help but blush although you really couldn't see the pink in my skin.

"Its fine Roel," he said taking one of my hands in his. "It probably would've happened even if you didn't hit her. She probably wouldn't have slapped me but it would've been somebody else."

"Oh," was all I could say. I didn't dare to make eye contact with him because I knew the feeling his eyes would give me. They made me feel small but protected. "Well your face is fine now," I said pulling my hand from his. "Do you still want me to cut your hair?"

I didn't hear his answer because thunder rolled extra loud over his voice. I looked towards the door with wide eyes. "I don't think it's a good time for that now," he said looking out the window.

The lights went out in the whole house and my body tensed. I quickly grabbed for Julian's hand while trying to adjust my eyesight.

"Scared of the dark," he asked in his smart ass tone.

"No," I said. I wasn't afraid of the dark but it always made me feel uneasy. "It's just something about being in the dark that makes me feel weird."

"Well can you see now," he asked getting up from the chair.

"A little, why," I asked.

"Because," he pulled up the hand I was holding, "I'm starting to lose feeling in my hand."

I let go of his hand quickly and mumbled "Sorry," to him.

"Good now I can take you upstairs," he said and grabbed my hand again.

I was startled that he was actually being nice to me. It felt good being with him when he's not in a bad mood. "So, how can you see so well?"

"Well I happen to always walk in the dark," he said. "I walk at night almost all of the time and it's not really hard to see around here."

"Oh, okay," I said following behind him while he led the way. "Why are you being so nice to me?"

He stopped in his tracks and turned to me. The only things I could see were his eyes. They were glowing in a dim orange glow. "Why do you insist on ruining the moment?"

"I wasn't trying to-"

"Well then just stop talking and walk," he said and turned around.

I was frozen in my feet. He hastily pulled me up the stairs and to my room. When we got to the door he left me there. The uneasy feeling I had when I was downstairs came back and I was started to feel scared.

"Julian, I hate you," I whispered still standing in the same place he left me. I walked into my room and was greeted with pitch blackness and cold air. A window was open on the other side of the room and the wind was creating a serious cold breeze. I walked over to the window and went to put it down when something caught my eye.

A man was standing on the ground below my window looking straight at me. His eyes were glowing in an eerie green color. He wasn't anyone from the house and he was freaking me out big time.

"Hey what are you doing," I yelled trying to be intimidating but it just came out as curiously scared.

I shouldn't have said anything because he started hovering above the ground. It was like he was flying. He was at my window within seconds.

I backed away quickly and fell over something that was on the floor. He came through my window and planted his feet on the ground.

"Who the hell are you," I yelled out of pure fear.

He got on his hands and knees and crawled toward me in lighting speed. His face was now inches from my face and I had hit my head on the bedpost.

I started to lose consciousness and he was finding it amusing. My eyes closed and I felt the hot liquid from my head pour down my neck. I heard the door open and a ball of white energy knocked the stranger out the window. I turned my head to see Chad standing there. His eyes weren't the normal dark grey.

They were black. I fell on the floor and let the darkness consume me.

I woke up with a booming headache. My vision was so blurry and it made my head hurt even more. I was lying in the living room with all five guys surrounding me. "What happened," I tried to say but the headache was over powering me.

"Don't talk Roel," Dean said putting a hand on my head. "You had a concussion and your skull is cracked a little."

I looked into his eyes and saw full concern and relief. "How long have I been out?"

"Almost four whole days," he said slowly. My eyes went wide and I tried to get up. "Ro rest," he said pushing me back down gently. I let myself fall back down and looked around.

Chad and Eric were crying and Julian had red rimmed eyes. Jared was sitting on the other side of the couch trying to look as if he wasn't happy I was awake.

"What about the house? Is it clean," I asked still aware of the fact that I had a job to do.

"The house is fine," Chad said walking over to me. "It was you we were worried about."

"You saved my life," I said trying to remember what happened. "The guy," I said remember the creepy stranger that was in my room four days ago, "there was a guy in my room. He tried to," I said not remembering what he tried to do. "And then Chad came and," shot out a ball of white energy at him, I finished the rest in my head.

Eric's eyes went completely wide and I knew he heard me.

"And what," Dean asked trying to get the rest of the info out of me. "And then what happened?"

"I forgot," I lied. "I can't remember what happened next. All I remember seeing before I passed out was Chad's face." I looked at Chad to see if he got what I was saying. *I saw his eyes Eric,* I thought. *I want answers.* He nodded his head signaling that he knew what I was talking about. "I-I want to rest. My head hurts badly."

"Okay guys let's leave her to rest," Julian started but I cut him off.

"Not everyone," I almost screamed. I flinched at how high my voice was. I was giving myself another headache. "I want Eric and Chad to stay."

"That's fine," Dean said. "Julian and Jared, you two come with me. We have business to take care of."

The three of them reluctantly exited the room and I was left with Chad and Eric.

"I want answers and I want them now," I said sitting up to get a better look at everything.

"What did you really see," Chad asked.

"I went to my room and my window was open. I went to close it and I saw a man below my window looking straight up at me. I went to ask him what he was doing and he flew into my bedroom. I fell and he got on all fours and crawled over to in two seconds. I hit my head and I think I screamed," I stopped to catch my breath and turned to Chad. "I saw you send a ball of energy towards him and he flew back out the window. Your eyes we—were black."

"So you remember everything," he asked.

"Don't change the subject, Chad. Tell me the truth," I said in a very cold tone.

"Well we're angels."

I started to laugh until I saw the seriousness in his eyes. "You're what," I asked choking back laughter.

"We're serious Ro," Eric said. "We're half angels and half-dragons."

I tried taking this in but it just didn't register in my head. "How is that possible?"

"Ask God," Chad said trying to make a joke out of the situation.

"Very funny, Chad but are you serious?" I couldn't wrap my finger around the whole thing. "So what are you two?"

"Well Eric is half angel and half flying dragon. He also has the element of air-"

"Wait, you can control the elements, too," I half yelled.

"Shhh, Roel," Chad said. "They can't know you know about us yet." He went to continue with what they were. "I'm half angel, half spirit dragon and I have the element of spirit. I can see dead people and actually communicate with them." I nodded my head to let him know I was listening. "Julian is half angel and half demon dragon which is a fire dragon. Well he is three-fourths demon dragon actually. That's why he's always so angry. He's different from all of us and he hates that. He also had the element of fire." That would explain why he is so freaking evil. "Dean is half angel half earth dragon. He has the element of earth." He laughed and looked at me. "Do I sound crazy to you?"

"Umm, n-no it's just so much to take in," I said looking at the ceiling. "What is Jared?"

"He's half angel, half water dragon. He has the element of water. I think that's why he's always so goofy."

"Oh," was all I could say. "Well I won't say I don't believe you because it explains a lot. I just need to think about it more. I think I'm still in shock." I looked up at the two of them and laughed. "Is there anything else-?"

"We have wings," Eric interrupted me. His body shifted and white wings came out of his back.

"What about that little slut," he said a tad bit too high. We both laughed and giggled at that remark. "She doesn't make him happy. I'd know since I know when he's lying."

"Oh," I said looking at my hands and fidgeting with my fingers. "Well he doesn't act happy when he's around me."

"Well you should feel what he's feeling," he said shaking his whole body.

"I don't think I want to know what he feels or what goes through his mind," I laughed. "So if you're my brother how were you born with them?"

"I wasn't born with them," he said. "I was put on their step. I didn't know mom that much. She obviously knew them because I was welcomed into the home with open arms from all of them. But this was almost fifty years ago so-"

"What," I yelled. "You guys are over fifty years old?!"

"Roel, stop yelling," he said putting his hand over my mouth. "They are over one hundred years old." I muffled words into his hand but he didn't move it. "I'm gonna move my hand. Can I trust you to not scream or yell?"

I nodded my head and he moved his hand. I tried to whisper as softly as I could, "How is it possible that I was born fifty years after you? Mom should've been dead by then."

"Mom was a," he started then stopped. He looked at me and covered his mouth as if he said too much.

"Chad," I said.

"She was a vampire."

I laughed hysterically. When I was done laughing I looked at him and smiled. "A vampire? Are you serious?"

He looked at me and frowned, "How else do you expect that she had another child at the age of seventy?"

"Seventy," I stressed. I should be running and screaming but for some reason I'm oddly calm and accepting about it. "She was old. Is there any reason I should think she was alive?"

"Most likely," he said. "She should be alive. Nothing can really kill her unless she stays in the sun for too long but I think that can kill anybody."

I laughed dryly. I started to feel slightly dizzy and very cold. I went to stand up and my body started to sway back and forth.

"Ro are you alright," Chad asked trying to grab my arm.

"I'm cold and dizzy," I said through my chattering teeth. He tried to walk me back to the couch but I didn't make it. I passed out at the entrance of the living room.

Before I blacked out completely I heard Chad scream, "Dean, get down here! She has wings!"

I woke of from one of the worst nightmares ever. I was three and our home was on fire house was on fire. We were sitting in the living room and I was sick during the time. I had this nasty cough and my body was so cold. I was sneezing and coughing that whole day. I sneezed one good time and a fire started in the kitchen. The stove and blew up and the kitchen was completely destroyed.

My mom ran me outside and went back to try to save the rest of the house. By the time the fire department came half of the house had collapsed. My mom was still inside but I knew she was just fine.

"Yea, you slept for twelve hours," he said. It was an awkward silence for a moment while everyone stared at me. Julian broke the silence, "What were you dreaming about because I couldn't get into your head at all?"

"And I couldn't read your mind," Eric chimed in.

"My mom," I said sadly. "I was having a nightmare about the day when she left me at the orphanage. I was sick and the house had caught up in flames. We made it out the house alive but she couldn't take care of me anymore. She left me there and I cried and scream myself to death. When they found me I was soaked to the bone because it was raining outside. They dragged me by my hair inside and I kicked and screamed. When they started to beat me I woke up."

"That had to be very painful to endure," Dean said from across the room.

"The beating up part or the losing my mom and house part," I asked rhetorically.

"Both," they all said at once and I laughed.

"I just wish I could've stayed with her. School would've been half bad," I said staring into the distance of the couch.

"How do you know that," Jared asked.

"I'm smart," I started. "I'm talented and I'm very athletic. When going to the orphanage I did all kinds of things. I drew all the time. I even drew a mural of the orphanage of me and my friends. Of course I got in trouble but it was fun."

"You went to school there," Dean asked.

"Sort of," I said. "We were put in age groups and we were put in the grade we were supposed to be in at that age. I was always put in a higher age group because I caught on so quickly."

"Well then," Dean said getting. "You will have to attend school if you plan on living here. We can enroll you in our school today. It's not too late."

"That's fine by me," I said.

"You would have to take a test so get dressed when you're feeling better and I'll meet you down here when you're ready," he said. He started to walk away but turned around. "Also you will need to start training you for flying and we need to find out what your element is." With that he walked out of the living room and went up to his room.

"You feeling okay," Julian asked from under me.

I totally forgot he was there and I quickly jumped off of him. "I'm fine now, thank you." I felt the blood rush to my face as I started to blush. Eric laughed lightly and I glared at him. "So umm, what should I wear for this test?"

"Anything you want to wear, Ro," Chad said taking my hand and walking me upstairs. We got to my room and he opened the door. "Do you want me to stay with until you get dressed?"

I looked around my room skeptically, "Yea I would like that," I said.

"Okay," he said.

I went into my room cautiously thinking that the earth demon would still be in here. I slowly walked over to my dresser and opened it. I had new apparel in each drawer. "Did you put my new clothes in here?"

Chad looked at me confused at first and then straightened up, "Oh yea I did that last night."

I nodded my head and turned back to my dresser. I pick out some underwear and a pair of light blue jeans with a white and black hello kitty shirt and went to the bathroom. I started getting undressed until I felt that same uneasy feeling I had when the saw the demon.

I looked around my bathroom and found a green piece of paper that was actually glowing. I went to the sink and picked it up. The uneasy feeling grew stronger and I started to feel sick. I read the piece of glowing green paper to myself:

Stay away from the White family or I will kill you. And that's a promise.

My head started spinning and I wanted to throw up. I ripped up the paper and threw it in the toilet and flushed it away.

I felt the uneasy feeling start to fade and the paper went down the drain. I was breathing heavy and I was hot. *How does anyone else know that I'm here?* I thought to myself.

I put the thought out of my head and took of the rest of my clothes. I turned on the water for the shower and stepped inside. The water felt so good against my skin. The heat was starting to create condensation on the doors of the shower. The steam was so relaxing. I could stay in here . . . . . All . . . . Night . . .

I felt myself drifting off into a deep sleep and I quickly washed up and got out. I looked in the mirror and just stared at my reflection. My skin looked completely healthier and darker than it was before yet I still looked pale. My unusual blue, black, and purple waves of hairs falling against my waist looked like the ocean. My big blue eyes were still hypnotizing.

"Roel are you okay in there," Chad asked from the other side of my door.

I jumped and squealed at the sound of his voice. "I'm fine," I yelled. "I'm getting dressed."

"Okay," he said as I heard him walking away from the door.

I heard more voices coming from the other of the door so I quickly got dressed and stepped out of the bathroom. What I didn't expect was to see Julian half-dressed sitting on my bed. I would have probably said something really rude to him but I was too infatuated with his smooth skin and perfect abs Chad was still there of course.

"Why are you staring at me like that," Julian asked. I shook myself out of the trance and walked over to him. I pointed to his chest and he looked down and smiled. "Oh," he said self-consciously, "I'll go put on a shirt."

"That wouldn't be necessary on my account," Chad said almost involuntarily.

"Actually it would be," I said pushing Julian out the door. I stopped when I realized just how less of an effect on him. I took my hands off his chest and stepped back. "Why did you come in here anyway," I asked putting my hands on my hips.

I smiled a little and crossed his arms. "I wanted to ask you if I could use your bathroom because Dean is occupying mine."

"Why mine?" I asked him suspiciously.

He laughed nervously and ran his fingers through his hair. "I used to use this bathroom before you came here."

I looked down at the floor and shook my foot nervously. I pointed my hand to the bathroom indicating that he can use it.

"Thanks," he said a little cold. He walked to the bathroom and turned back to me and smiled evilly. "I hope you have air freshener," he said and walked into the bathroom.

"You're sick," I said as he shut the door behind him. I looked at Chad who was staring at the empty space where Julian just had been. "Can you stop looking at him like he's food?"

He looked at me and smiled, "I'll try but I can't promise you anything." He laughed until he realized he was the only one laughing. "I think he's hot, so what?

He was a nice guy to be around. He was always there when I passed out. He just seemed so brotherly to me.

"Thanks Ro," he smiled.

"No problem, Dean," I said back and turned my attention back out the window.

The sun was shining bright and the sky looked gorgeous. The town was made up of small buildings and tall skyscrapers, nothing in between. We drove past plenty of parks, school and shopping plazas. Being able to actually see these things freely brought much joy to my heart. I thought I was going to cry from overwhelming happiness.

"You can call me D.W," Dean said out of the blue making me look at him in confusion. "My mom used to call me that before she left." He looked sad for a moment but then brushed it away.

"I'm so sorry to hear that," I said quietly, "about your mom, not the nickname."

"I know," he said saving me from humiliation. "We all had nicknames from her. She called Chad C.W. Jared was called Jay or junior. He was named after our father. Eric was always called E.J. he was named after our grandfather. Julian had a funny nickname. Ju-ju is what mom called him." We laughed for a second. "If she was to meet you then Ro would be your name."

"O," I said. "Why didn't you guys keep your names after your mom left?"

"We tried to do it for a while but it didn't last very long. It always ended with one of us depressed. And when one of us is depressed, the entire town pays for it." He said.

No pressure. "Why are you gonna let me call you by that name?" I asked concerned.

"Well," he started mostly focusing on the road ahead of him. "You remind me of my mother, personality wise. You always stand up to Julian for others and that's what she always did. When we took in Chad, she was ecstatic." He stopped and looked over to see if I was following. I nodded for him to keep going.

"She never let Julian talk about Chad," she said. "She would always say something smart to him to make him angry and send him stomping off to his room." He laughed lightly to himself. "When she left, we were lost. We didn't know how to control Julian," he started to look distant. "We fight all the time, now."

"Well at least you know how it feels to have a mom," I said absently.

"O, sorry," he apologized. "Here I am crying over having a mother that just left when you don't even know yours."

"Hey it's alright," I said back smiling. "It's not like she didn't want me in the first place. She couldn't take care of me anymore due to the fire. Come to think of it, I might have started the fire."

At this point I figured we were just driving around but I wasn't upset about that. I was out of the house and I was able to vent to someone about my feelings.

"So you think your element if fire?"

"Maybe," I said. "Well I'm really not sure what it is but I can't wait to find out."

"Me to, sis," he said, "Me too." He smiled at me and took my hand.

I felt so wanted for the first time in forever but I had to figure out one thing. "You're not taking me to the school, are you?"

He laughed and took the wheel again. "We start school in two weeks. Eric told me about you and school already. I got you set up for school the day we went out."

I looked out the window and smiled to my reflection. "Thank you then," I said.

"For what," he asked puzzled.

they were crazy. I slowly stepped out of the car and to where they were standing.

I scared myself half to death by looking over the cliff and to the little line of the river that was about two hundred feet below us. "Wha-what the hell are you guys doing," I asked shaking a little.

"We're flying," Eric said shooting out his wings and gracefully lifting his body off the ground.

Each of them, except for Julian, started to fly off the cliff. Julian just turned and looked at me.

"Be calm and breathe," he whispered putting his hand around my waist.

"Okay," I said as his hand left an electric tingle where it touched me.

"Think of something happy," he started. "Close your eyes and think of a happy moment in your life."

I started to think the first time I met Julian and how he was the most gorgeous creature I've ever laid eyes on. I felt a tug at the skin on my back and soon darkness covered us.

"Open your eyes," Julian said startling me. "Your wings are out.

I opened my eyes to see my wings cocooning us. I opened my wings and everyone was staring at us causing me to blush wildly.

"It's okay," Julian said and held his hand out as his wings slowly came out of his back. "Take my hand."

I looked at his hand and then into his eyes. The vulnerability was back in then and I felt my heart twinge for him. He was back to being nice to me and I was going to take it while I can. I grabbed his hand and walked toward the edge of the cliff with him.

"Are we really gonna jump off this cliff," I asked in a shaky voice.

"No," he said sarcastically, "we're gonna walk down the side of it."

"Sarcasm is not your forte."

He gave me a look indicating that I was ruining the happy moment. So he smiled and jumped off the cliff with my hand still in his.

I let out an ear piercing scream before it registered that I did have wings.

When I felt myself soaring through the sky instead of plummeting to the ground I opened my eyes to a beautiful horizon. The sky was completely blue and it mirrored the beautiful blue and green water below us.

I felt content and I was flying perfectly. Julian was hesitant to let my hand go but I wanted to feel the breeze between my fingers. I closed my eyes and relaxed in the breeze that was caressing my entire body. I felt like I was on top of the world.

I started humming my favorite song, Don't Let Me Go by The Fray, and felt myself relax completely. I swear people were talking to me but I didn't hear it.

"Ro, we have to come down," I heard a voice say but I couldn't put a face to it.

"Okay," I said with a sigh. A hand covered mine and I felt a soft shock run through my body. I knew who that was and a smiled crept across my face.

When we came to the ground I opened my eyes to the most beautiful lake I have ever seen, well the only lake I've ever seen. The water was completely clear and you could see the fish and sea creature swimming beneath the surface.

Jared walked over to the lake and started to freeze it. I yelled for him to wait.

"What about the fish and stuff," I asked shocked that he was about to freeze living things.

He laughed and grabbed my hand, "Sweetheart, look at this," he started to freeze the lake but the fish were still swimming. "I only froze enough for us not to fall in."

I felt a little stupid to think he would kill animals. "Oh," was all I could say. "So how are we going to skate without skates?"

He sat down next to the lake and with his hand and element he made what looked like ice skating skates on the bottom of his shoes. He pulled me to the ground next to him and did the same to mine.

A few minutes went by before he had everyone's shoes looking like skates. All five of them went across the lake gracefully and I just stood there like an idiot. I forgot I didn't know how to do this. I slowly walked on the frozen surface thinking that my athleticism would help me out but to my surprise, note the sarcasm, I fell flat on my ass.

"Ow," I laughed and laid back on the cold surface that was actually completely relaxing.

"Are you okay?" Chad had come to my rescue but it was not needed.

I closed and smiled. "Yeah," I breathed. "I'm athletic but I'm not coordinated."

"We can see that," Julian said skating over to me. I gave him a rude gesture causing him to roar with laughter. "Hey, it looks like my jerkiness is finally rubbing off on you."

"Don't get too happy, Julian," I said. "I've always been an asshole but you guys bring the best out of me."

"Nice," he said seductively. "Damn it Chad," he yelled and pushed Chad over.

"What did I do," Chad said fighting with the laughter that was building in his chest.

"Chad you're interrupting my mellow," I whispered peeking up at him.

He suppressed a giggle and said, "Sorry."

I smiled at him and closed my eyes again. I lifted myself up and started to skate again. This time I got the hang of it and didn't fall on my ass. I started to try some tricks and managed to stay vertical which was a plus. I felt like I was flying again and it felt good. I was at peace as you could see. Nothing was going to change my mood.

I was gliding gracefully when a force of uneasiness fell over me. I lost my footing and almost fell on my face. Thank goodness I was in a happy moment because my wings flew out as quickly as I fell and I was in the air.

I looked around for my five men and found them looking up at me in pure shock. "What's wrong," I went to ask but it came out as a ferocious roar. I almost pissed in my pants, if I were wearing any.

I looked down to the surface of the lake and a great white dragon was staring back at me. My voice screamed in my head but a loud high pitched roar came out of my mouth. I started to panic when fire and water came out of my mouth at the same time.

What the hell is wrong with me, I thought to myself while I freaked out and roared.

Just then, Chad shifted and shook under his skin. A black dragon burst from the place where he stood and it freaked me out even more. He flew toward and I tried my hardest not to freak out.

Roel, can you hear me, Chad thought to me.

I was still mentally screaming but I clearly heard his voice as if he said it in my ear. *YES, WHAT THE HELL HAPPENED?*

YOU TURNED INTO A DRAGON, he said as if this was something that happened every day. *Can you tell me why you almost fell on your face and turned yourself into a dragon?*

I felt an uneasy feeling like something was watching me and it wasn't-, I started to feel uneasy again and I saw something flicker from across the lake. I looked over and saw the glowing bright green eyes that haunted

room due to the ivy," he said looking at the lotion. "I was getting pretty bored just standing at your door for the past three days."

What do you say to something like that? Wait . . . did he just say he stood in front of my door for three days? Was he on some type crack that made him bipolar or was just part his personality?

"Well my skin is getting better," I started. My skin was still red, redder than it should have been. I'm the color of peanut butter so I shouldn't get red. Most of the rash went away I was just left with scratch marks and red bruises. "Thanks for the lotion though."

I ran out of Calamine lotion last night and I was in serious of a rub down. Normally Chad would come in and assist me when Dean wasn't around.

"Do you need any help putting it on your back," he blurted out. He instantly cringed and I giggled.

"Sure," I said through subtle laughter. "You know it's not a crime to be nice right?" I turn my back toward him indicating that he can start applying the cold Calamine lotion to my back.

He hesitated to touch me but relaxed when he started rubbing on the lotion on my upper back. "I know but it's just really hard for me. I've been around them forever so they became used to me being an asshole." He worked his down my back and I fought back the urge of my eyes fluttering shut. "And when you came along and I was an ass you didn't take it from me. You stood up for Chad and called me a dick several times. It's getting harder to be mean to you because you show me what I am through everyone else's eyes. You shoot the attitude back at me and it's frustrating because you don't hold your tongue for anyone."

I don't know it I should like what he's saying or be offended. "Is that a good thing or a bad thing?"

He stopped rubbing my back and put his arms around me and threw me on the bed. "I'm still trying to figure that out believe it or not," he said into the back of my head.

I smiled thankful he couldn't see how red my face was. I turned to face him and looked into his eyes. The beauty of his eyes grabbed a hold of me. When they say the 'beauty is in the eye of its beholder', they weren't lying because the creature that was staring back at me was beyond beautiful.

"Why are you staring at me like that," he asked softly. His voice was like silk running against my skin and it was hard not to closed my eyes and breathe in his scent.

"You amaze me in more ways than one," I said slowly. "I mean, you can be the angriest person in the house and then you turn into this complete sweetheart that smiles and has soft eyes with so much vulnerability in them." I paused to catch my breath. "As frustrating as it is I find it interesting. I understand what makes you angry but you have to know that it was in the past."

He pinched the bridge of his nose with his finger and I thought the closed off Julian was back. "Roel," he whispered. "I've tried to get over it many times and you saying make it that much easier to let it go."

"You mean just because I said that you're gonna let it go," I asked curiously.

He laughed humorlessly and said, "Yes that is what I mean." He pulled me closer to him and kissed my forehead.

"Hold on Julian," I said pushing against his chest. "What about Julia?"

He pointed to the light scars on his face. "I am no longer dating her due to a beautiful angel that interrupted my life in the best way."

"I hope that angel has ocean blue eyes," I said and smiled at him.

"I think her eyes are gorgeous," he said and lightly flicked my nose.

I giggled softly and looked at my overly exposed thin body. I didn't want to be serious but I had to ask an important question. "Why did you hate me when I first came here? You were rude to me and loved to watch me squirm under your tall body. What did I do to you?"

His body went stiff and I thought he stopped breathing. I looked up to find him watching me intently. "I have never seen anything so beautiful and amazing since my mom left. She's like you in every sense. Though you two look nothing alike you make me think about her all the time. I thought I would never fall in love because no one was like my mother. I was feeling like no one could give me what my mom gave me. She was strict, stern, sweet, loving, caring," he paused to laugh and said, "bitchy." I giggled with him. "She stood up for Chad when nobody would take him in or care for him. She didn't take shit from anybody.

"And then you came along and I felt her again when I saw you. You made me feel as though I was looking right at her through another's person's eyes. I felt like she was sending me something that she made just for me. She and God made you just for me. I didn't like the feeling because I felt like I was going to get my heart broken again. She left me and I thought that you would leave.

"When you were dreaming and said that I hurt you enough and you were leaving I thought you were gonna leave altogether. I was scared that when I wake up you wouldn't be there and it would be my fault. I don't know what I'm feeling for you but I like every bit of it. I can't go a day without thinking about you and if you're okay.

I thought I was going to die when you didn't wake for four days. It was my fault then too.

Where the hell did all that come from? Is he confessing his feelings toward me? What do you say to that? *Find words, Roel,* I thought to myself. *SAY SOMETHING YOU IDIOT.* "I love you," I blurted out. *WHAT THE HELL WAS THAT! DID YOU REALLY JUST SAY THAT? ROEL ZOEY SOMERS ARE YOU FREAKING INSANE!*

His body went stiff again and I couldn't bear to look in his eyes. "I guess those were better and easier words than everything I just said," he said with light laughter. Is he saying what I think he's saying? "I love you too."

I think I stopped breathing and the world just didn't matter at all. "Huh," was all I could manage to get out at the time. "You mean it?"

"Yea I mean it," he said putting his finger under my chin to make me look at him. When I did look at him a tear fell down my face. "Why are you crying?" He went to kiss my tear from my face.

"You are the first person in fourteen years to tell me they love me," I said slowly because I didn't want my voice to crack or quiver.

"Then I hope those are good tears," he said his eye watering a little.

Julian is as tough as he makes himself. He's just a young, well old young child wanting to be loved by someone. And I want to be the one to bring down the walls around his heart, mind and soul.

I don't know how long Julian and I sat there but I surely didn't complain. The way I feel about him complicates things completely. I didn't know if what I was saying was true or if it was a reaction to everything he said. I'm still trying to figure out why those three words came out of my mouth.

"What are you thinking about," he asked me quietly. He was holding me and stroking my hair absently.

I looked into his soft orange eyes and felt almost complete. "You," I said in a whisper. He's making me think that I really do love him and that I really want to be with him. "Everything you just told me was completely breathtaking. I don't know what to say to that."

"Say what's on your mind, Roel," he said looking at me more intently. "You have to be feeling something."

"I am feeling something," I argued softly. "I just don't know how to put it in words." I can tell him that I love him but I can't express why I love him. I've only known him for two weeks, three weeks tops, and I don't know everything about him. What about him do I love so much?

I looked deeply into his eyes to find the words. "Your eyes," I blurted out. "They can be so hard and angry and then when you look at me like that," I pointed to the soft and sweet expression that was now spreading across his face, "your eyes are as soft as the blanket that is now under us. I can take the bipolar issues because I have my moments too but I just can't get enough of your issues.

"We're both damaged and I know that I may be more damaged than you are but that gives me reason to fall in love and find a family." Damaged wasn't even the word for what I am. I am far from the word. I am beyond repair as of this moment. "I want to find something that doesn't include people hurting me or making me feel inferior." I fell in love with the person that has been hurting me but that's life. "You love the ones that hurt you and hurt the ones that love you. It's the fucking circle of life," I had to stop myself from babbling.

"I hope everything I said made sense because I don't know how to explain the reason why I love you."

"I think you explained yourself pretty well," he said still pushing my hair behind my ear absently. "I think I like what you said."

A lot of banging came from the other side of the door before Chad and Dean came bursting through it. "Did I not tell you that she was to be alone," Dean screamed at Julian causing him to jump off the bed and run towards him.

"Dean it isn't that serious," Chad said getting between the two fuming boys.

"Why can't you just listen," Dean said ignoring Chad and pushing him out the way to get to Julian. "Did you forget that poison ivy is contagious?"

"It would be worth it to be with her alone," Julian said through his teeth. "You keeping her in here like a freaking prisoner isn't gonna help the fact that she needs to heal."

"What if you or Chad got poison ivy," he yelled back. "We have school in a week and you guys want to risk starting because of some girl."

Ouch, I am standing right here you know. "Some girl Dean," I said in a whisper. Just a few days ago he was calling me his sister and saying I remind him of his mother. What the hell is with these boys and their bipolar issues? "What the hell is up with you? When did I become just some girl to you, Dean? When did I change from being your sister, the one you call Ro, to just some girl."

"You don't understand, Roel," he said through his teeth.

"Then help me understand, Dean," I yelled. "Help me understand why I have to be treated like shit from everyone I love. Help me understand your change in attitude so fast. Help me understand why you're treating me like a diseased patient in a hospital because I just don't understand anything."

"I don't have to explain myself to you," he sneered. "You're a worthless rat and I could care less what happens to you."

Low blow that really hurt more than anything I've ever heard. "Good," I said in a shaky voice. "Now I know your true feelings. Thanks *bro* for the truth and actually letting me see you true colors." I turned my head toward my window to block the anger and sadness that was building up in my chest. "I need to go for a walk," I said. I put on some shorts and brushed past the three fuming men.

"What the hell is your problem," Julian and Chad yelled. I didn't wait to hear the rest of their conversation.

Before I knew it I was out the door and flying through the trees. Thankfully I didn't turn into a dragon because I would've been shot down or something.

I flew for what seemed like hours. I cried and screamed and yelled relieving the anger frustration and sadness that wouldn't stop flowing from my chest.

My wings got tired and I dropped next to a flowing stream. I didn't have the energy to put my wings back so I just left them. I pulled my knees to my chest and wrapped my arms around them.

I sat there and cried for hours. It was dark before I knew it and I needed to get home. I didn't want to go back but I knew I had to. I had to be there for Julian and Chad. They were probably worried sick. Or maybe they felt the same way Dean felt and it was just a setup to get me to leave.

If that was true then everything Julian said was a lie. And Chad wasn't even my brother. I wanted to cry even more but I didn't have any more water in my body. I was far too angry to think of crying anymore.

"Roel," a soft voice said from behind me. The only person that wasn't an asshole, the only person that was true to me from the start, was Eric.

I turned and ran to him and cried on his shoulder. "Eric," I whispered his name softly still weeping. "Why me?"

He shushed me and gently stroked my hair, "It's okay, it's okay," he said softly into my hair. "I'm right here Ro. I'm not going anywhere." He hugged me a little more before putting my hands around his waist and lifting us up in the air.

I didn't care where we went or what we were doing because I was in the arms of an angel. He came to my rescue and that is all I needed to know. I didn't care that he followed me for that matter. He knew the pain I was in. He knew I couldn't manage this pain alone.

Before I knew it I was hugging my pillow and lying on Eric's chest. He didn't give me butterflies like when I was with Julian but I felt something. I felt genuine caring and love radiating off of Eric. He cared for me just as much as Chad or Julian. I don't love him like I love Julian but he's my best friend.

We laid there for hours before the sun started to rise. He slept but when I would sniffle or start to cry he would absently caress my hair or rub my arm for support. I was safe in his arms and I knew it. But how long would Dean let me stay if he didn't like me anymore?

Chapter 6

I was getting ready for school when a soft knock interrupted me. "Come in," I said already knowing who it was.

"Hey," Eric said. "Are you ready to go?"

I had on a plaid, pink, black and white, button up tunic with flower fishnet leggings and plaid black and white Chuck Taylor All Stars on. I looked myself over for the tenth time and sighed. I let down my hair and let it cascade down my back. "Yes I'm ready."

"Thankfully we don't have to wear uniform huh," he said knowingly. "You wouldn't be able to show off your style."

I laughed and said, "I wouldn't even wear the stupid uniform if we had one." I grabbed my shoulder pink and black skull bag that said "I kill sparkly things and snuggle under warm furry things."

"I bet," he said laughing. Ever since Dean did what he did Eric has been there for me. He helped me with the ending of my poison ivy. He's been the only one that could enter my room. We went on a long walk yesterday so I could clear my head about school. I told him I wanted to walk to school and he couldn't be happier.

We walked downstairs to find everyone sitting on at the island in the kitchen. I haven't even talked to Julian or Chad. Eric and Jared are the only ones that I've been able to talk to. I felt bad only because Chad and Julian didn't do anything. But I just couldn't face them right now.

"Morning Ro," Jared said coming to hug me. "I hope you had a good sleep. I made breakfast this morning so don't worry about it."

"Thanks Junior," I said hugging him back. "Good morning Julian, Chad," I said hugging the both of them.

Chad jumped up and down like a girl who just got asked to prom. "Morning Ro," he screeched. "I thought you would never talk to me again."

"Me too," Julian said sarcastically throwing my hand off of him.

Why am I not surprised? He told me that he loved me and I said it back and then I stop talking to him for a week. I would be angry too.

"I see the asshole is back," I said smugly. "I was starting to think that I was getting special treatment."

He snorted and stood up. "You are no special than anyone else in this house," he said putting his dishes in the sink. "You're the maid remember."

So I've been hanging out with Eric who has the element of air. He taught me some things and I was in a mood to use them. I raised my hands and the dishes started to clean themselves. "I am the maid but I won't be cleaning your dishes."

I sat down to eat my breakfast and found I was eye to eye with Dean. The pain in my chest erupted but I kept the tears back and the anger in control.

"Roel," he said in a short clipped tone.

My appetite was gone when I saw his face. "Dick," I snipped back. I got up from the island and turned to Chad Eric and Jared. "Are you walking with us Jared?"

"Of course," he said in a matter of fact tone. "I'm not like these assholes," he pointed to Dean and Julian. "Let's go."

Jared, Chad, Eric and I walked out the house and strolled to school. The two dick-wads trailed behind us and muttered to each other about how much of a bitch I was acting. Hey it takes one to know one right?

"So what kind of competition do I have here," I asked.

"There are many girls here," Jared stated. "But none of them can compare to our black hair and blue eyed beauty."

I started to blush and hid my face in Eric's chest. "Jared," I said all childish and embarrassed. "You're making me blush."

He put his arm around me and kissed the side of my forehead. "Only for you my sweet," he said into the side of my head.

Jared has feelings for me and I know it but I can't reciprocate them. I'm still in love with the orange eyed monster walking a few yards behind us. For the love of God why won't he go away?

The walk to school was surprisingly short and I was thankful for that. I didn't get much sleep last night due to the nervousness of going to a public school and the nightmares I was having. I haven't had a good night's sleep in a while.

The school was huge, gigantic, colossal; I don't know any other words to use. It had to be at least two miles long if a school can get that big. It looked like any other school just a few times bigger.

We were walking up to the entrance when a few girls past us. "Hey Jared," they said in unison.

I'm guessing Jared was one of the ladies men. "Hey girls," he said and kissed the side of my head again.

He was being an ass to them but I didn't care. No girl is worthy of my guys without my approval.

We walked to the office to get my schedule and books. It didn't take long for them to give me what I need and assign me to my locker which was between Julian and Dean, oh the joy, note the sarcasm. Thankfully Julian switched lockers with me so I was next to Eric. That was better except for the fact that I was still next to Julian.

I looked at my schedule and saw that I had math first. Math and art were my favorite subjects. I was a big fan on pre-calculus, algebra and art history.

Thankfully I have all my classes with Chad but not thankful because I have all my class with Julian. Dean in a sense was a senior so I didn't share any classes with him. I had two classes with Jared and Eric which was another plus.

Chad and I walked to Algebra together with Julian behind us. "Ms. Ian is the best teacher," Chad said. "I had her my first year. She loves math just as much as any mathematician. You'll like her."

I smiled nervously, "I hope so."

We sat in the very back and I was sandwiched between Julian and Chad. Why must he torture me like this? What did I do to deserve his presence as of this moment?

As if my day couldn't get any worse a familiar face walked in the classroom. If God wanted to torture me he could just smite me instead of the ongoing anger that was now building in my chest.

"Hi Julian," Julia said in a high pitched voice. She pranced over to us flipping her hair in the process. "Hey, rainbow butt and cunt sucker," she said without even looking our way.

I went to my seat and nudged Chad in the gut for making me go up there. "Dude you so suck right now," I whispered harshly.

He squirmed and rubbed his side. "I'm sorry I didn't know you didn't like an audience," he said with a smile.

"Now class we turn our attention to the physics of Algebra," Ms. Ian said writing variables and numbers on the board.

Let the fun of math begin.

School was like something I couldn't imagine. The only word I could use was boring. English and History were the deadest classes I could go through. The teachers lectured like they were college professors. The classes were a little over an hour long but I couldn't take it I was so ready for lunch.

"So how was your first day, Ro," Jared asked me while we were sitting outside on the grass for lunch. I was glad they brought a blanket because the ground was still wet from the previous days of rain.

I was lying down on the blanket looking toward the sky with Chad and Eric on either side of me. "It was so boring," I said quietly. I looked over toward him to see that he was not alone. "So you brought the orange asshole with you. I thought he was with his barbie doll girlfriend."

Julian snorted and mumbled something under his breath but I couldn't hear it. He's such an ass hat. "I hope you're having a nice day too twerp," he said to me.

I laughed sarcastically and said, "I'm having a better day than you are I bet."

"You bet," he said sitting next to Chad. He just makes me so sick I can't even stand it.

"Whatever," I said under my breath. "Jared, how was your day?"

"I missed you," he said pushing Eric over and sitting next to me. "Girls were all over me but I had to tell them that I was taken."

"Who's the lucky girl," I teased. "Jared you know we're not together."

"I know," he said moving hair from my face, "but the girls in school don't know that."

"We know that," Julian said with rude sarcasm.

I sat up and gave him an innocent look. "Is someone jealous," I asked.

He gave me a disgusted look. "In your dreams, orphan" he spat.

"You wish, demon," I smirked.

"Ouch," Chad teased. "Julian take a chill pill we know you love Ro."

I punched Chad as Julian said, "I don't love her!"

I froze mid-punch and looked at Julian. He had a look of regret on his face.

"Good to know," I said as I got up and walked away.

Just as I walked away Dean walked past me. "Roel," he said.

"Asshole," I retorted. "I'll be leaving the house in a week. No need to give a shit about me."

"What are you talking about," Dean yelled as I kept walking away. "Where are you gonna go?"

"What does it matter," I yelled back as I made my way to Art.

"Ro would you just stop and listen," Julian yelled grabbing my arm.

"Listen to you lie to me again," I yelled snatching my arm away from him. "I don't think so."

I've been walking around since I left lunch and class doesn't start for another ten minutes. Julian and Chad followed me to make sure I didn't leave the school. Why Julian came, I don't know and I didn't want anything to do with him.

"Roel stop," Chad said standing in front of me. "You're not leaving me so don't even think about it."

I looked into his eyes as tears stained my cheeks. "What makes you think I want to stay now? Dean and Julian are being dicks and I'm sick of it!"

"Hey," he said pulling me into a hug. "Someone once told me that when someone is talking about you or being mean, you call them a dick and walk away with your head held high."

"I know,' I laughed into his shoulder. "I just don't want to be treated like shit from them."

He kissed my head and said, "What can we do if they're natural ass hats and brain challenged dickheads?"

I laughed and Julian coughed. "I'm still standing here," he said pointing to himself.

"Why are you here," I asked with a disgusted look on my face. He went to say something but I stopped him. "I'm not gonna stick around just so you and Dean can keep up with this bipolar bullshit. So from now on even if you guys don't speak to me, I will be most happy if you don't, you will respect me and the rest of this family." I gave him a stern look and he shrunk into himself. "I will not take any more shit out of you two, am I clear?"

He looked like a little boy who just got caught watching his dad's porn. "Understood," he said softly.

"Good," I said with a little more confidence in myself. "Now, Chad, walk me to class," I said and Chad and I walked away.

Art was my favorite class by far. It was a simple class but when you love art that is how it is supposed to be. It was my release and I loved every minute of it, except for the eerie feeling I'm starting to get.

Something was wrong and it wasn't just because Julian and his artificial freak, Julia, were in the class.

"Ok class," the teacher said as he walked in the class. Something about him was familiar. "I'm your new teacher, Mr. Lee."

His eyes, they were familiar. They gave me that eerie feeling. I remember those eyes. They were the eyes that haunted my dreams and nightmares for the last few weeks. This cannot be happening.

The love I have for Art flew out the window when the earth demon entered the room.

Chapter 7

So school was just not for me. I hated every part of it. I shared all my classes with Julian. His bitch of an ex-girlfriend wanted me to rip her throat out. Julian doesn't love me anymore. And on top of all of that, I have an earth demon for my favorite class of all time, and for gym. My life was just getting worse by the minute.

Thankfully the principal gave me all independent classes due to the fact that I was smarter than the average junior or senior high school student. I never have to attend class but I have to come to school until lunch.

"I just can't believe the day I've had," I said to no one as I jumped face first on my bed. I knew I had to get up and do work but I didn't want to do anything at the moment.

A booming knock followed by Julian made me even worse. "There's someone at the door for you," he spat at me.

"Who would be at the door for me Julian," I said into my pillow.

"Mr. Lee," he said leaning against the doorway. "He is rather upset that you walked out of class today. By the way what made you walk out?"

"I have my reasons," I said as I got up from my bed and pushed past him and went downstairs. "Why don't you mind your business," I yelled as he followed me all the way to the door.

"I have to see you get in trouble," he said smugly. "I need to know you're as pathetic as I thought you were."

I turned and slapped him across that gorgeous face of his. "I told you I wasn't taking any of your bullshit." I put my finger his face which was stuck in a shocked expression. "Take your rude pathetic ass back upstairs and leave me the hell alone," I snipped at him.

Slowly he retreated back upstairs before I was greeted with an uneasy feeling. I turned into the living room and was greeted by those terrible green eyes that were engraved in my mind.

"Why the hell are you here," I asked standing behind by the stairs and not making any attempt to get any closer.

"Fear not my sweet angel," he said in an eerily sweet tone. "I am here on a friendly visit seeing as I am you art and gym teacher."

"What is friendly when you've already tried to kill me twice," I asked in a sadistic tone.

"You must forgive my actions my dear," he said sitting down on the couch.

For a moment I actually looked at him. His dark brown hair was pulled into a ponytail and he had soft pale skin. His lips were full and pink. He was exceedingly taller than me making me look like a smurf. He was handsome except for the eerie feeling his eyes gave me.

"So why are you here," I said sitting in the single chair. I was getting dizzy and I knew I couldn't stand by the stairs anymore.

"Well as you know I have this feud with your fellow roommates," he said crossing his legs. "And you know that in order for them to survive I have to kill you right?"

The uneasy feeling went away and it was replaced with rage. "Get the hell out of my house," I said in a controlled tone.

"Well it would suffice that I kill the only part of their coven that they really truly need," he said not budging from his spot.

"Get out," I said getting up from my chair. I left my hair start to rise and flames engulfed my hands.

He got up from his spot and started backing up to the door. "I will complete my task and the prophecy will not be fulfilled."

He didn't make it out the door before a ball of flames hit him in the chest. "I SAID GET OUT!" my voice shook the entire house.

"What the hell is going on," Dean yelled coming down the stairs. I turned toward he and he stopped in his tracks. "Roel what's wrong?"

The rage that was boiling in me didn't subside and I let a roaring scream. It shook the house and cut off all the lights. When my voice was hoarse I fell to the ground in the fetal position.

Chad Eric and Jared ran to my side in an instant. "What happened," Chad said pulling me into a hug.

"Earth . . . Demon," I said through gritting teeth. I went from being extra hot to being freezing cold. "The . . . Prophecy . . . ," I said looking at Dean.

"We'll talk about it later," he said taking me from Chad and taking me upstairs. "Chad, Eric, Julian, put up some wards around the house so that the demons can't enter. Jared, come with me."

"What's going on," I mumbled. "What is the pro-?"

"Not right now Roel," he whispered as we entered my room. "Jared, make sure all of the windows are closed check the bathroom," he yelled over his shoulder to Jared who obeyed without question.

He put me on my bed and I impatiently struggled to pull the covers over me. My eyes were getting heavy and I couldn't fight the blackness that was covering my sight. "I . . . don't . . . want . . . to . . . pass . . . out . . . again," I said through clenched teeth.

"You'll be fine," Dean said caressing my hair. "You wasted a lot of your energy with what you did so you need to rest."

I didn't want to sleep but my eyes were telling Dean and everyone else that entered the room a different story. "Fine," was the last thing I said before fell asleep?

Everything was green. Everything. Nothing was right. Everything about this dream was wrong. Nothing about this dream was real. And there were those eyes.

His eyes appeared in the trees. I could see the eerie green in front of the dark green trees. His face started to appear and I had nowhere to run.

I sucked it up and shouted at him. "Why do you insist on bothering me," I attempted to put confidence in my voice but it cracked.

"I told you what I wanted," he whispered. His voice sending chills down my spine. He appeared in front of me and snaked his hands around my neck. "You may have the power to keep me away when you're awake but you're dreaming now and I control you."

"That's where you're wrong ass hat," a voice said from behind me. Before I knew it an orange ball of energy went through me and burst into the demons chest. "I control these dreams."

I turned to see a very angry god making his way toward us. To my relief I was looking at Julian. I smiled but it was cut short due to the fact that he was glowing orange and scaring the hell out of me.

"Roel wake up," he said putting his hand on my shoulder.

I instantly shot upright out of the dream. "Julian," I screamed. "Julian!" I ran out the door and ran straight into the arms of my love.

"Roel I'm fine," he said into my hair as we fell on the floor. "It's okay," he said caressing my hair.

"I'm so scared," I said into his chest. I didn't realize I was crying until I saw that his shirt was stained with salt water.

"Don't be," he whispered into ear. "I'm here with you. You never have to be afraid."

"What the hell is going on," Dean said coming out of his room. "Is she okay?"

"He came into her dream and tried to suffocate her in her sleep," Julian said pulling us off the floor. "He thought he was the only one that could come into her dreams."

I didn't let him go because I couldn't stand on my own. I was scared but I was also angry. "What the hell is this prophecy about and what does it have to do with me?"

Dean pinched the bridge of his nose and said, "Roel, it's the middle of the night-"

"Damn it Dean," I yelled. Everyone was out in the hallway already. "I don't give a shit what time it is and apparently neither do the demons that are trying to kill me. I don't want to hear this sissy ass excuse the time is not right! A demon almost killed me in my sleep and you still want to keep this damn prophecy a secret?" I started to heat up but my hands didn't become balls of flame. Instead the air around me swirled and lifted my hair. "I'm getting pissed," I yelled.

Dean embraced me. "Okay," he said. "Can you please stop wasting your energy?"

I calmed down and the air around me subsided. "Let me go," I said in a controlled tone. I was still pissed at him so it wasn't helping me that he was holding me.

He let me go and they all lead me downstairs. We sat in the living room, Jared and Eric sat on the floor. Julian and Chad were on the couch and Dean stood. I sat in the single chair. The same chair that I sat in earlier.

"Well since you are asking for so much right now," Dean started. I gave him a look that conveyed how tired I was of his bullshit and he had better get on with his bullshit. "Getting on with the story. Our kind is dying away. I mean the winged angels and part dragons. The earth demon that is trying so hard to kill you is one of the reasons that our race is dying."

"Are you telling me there are more of those demons," I asked.

"Unfortunately, yes," he continued. "When you read all those stories and here about all those mythology legends there's always a good and evil. The bible has God and Lucifer which has Heaven and Hell. Mythology has Zeus and Hades which has Olympus and the Underworld. There are so much more places and names I can say but that would be beating around the bush.

"We are the good people of our kind. Granted we are also demons but that is only because of that fact that we are part dragon. The demons that are trying to kill you are part snake which is basically full demon. There are many more kinds of species of us but they are almost non-existent." He looked at me and I was sure I had a clueless expression on my face. "Are you keeping up?" I nodded waved for him to continue.

"Well the prophecy was said that an angel with pure white angel wings and the ability to conjure all elements will be the end of all the snake demons. The army of that angel will be able to conjure one of the five elements each. That's where we come in.

"As you know we all can manipulate each element and you are showing signs of all the elements. You also have pure white wings. When Chad found you it wasn't only because you were his sister and we needed a maid. We had been searching and tracking someone who we thought was the perfect person. When we found out that it was a girl Chad knew just where to look.

"The prophecy had been coming true for the past fifty years and now things are changing. The demons are growing stronger and our race is growing weak. We need something new that will help us kill these bitch ass demons. That's where you come along."

So I'm a big part of some damn prophecy. I'm the biggest part of the prophecy. I have the power to kill all these demons. I'm the one that they have been searching for. I'm the missing piece to the puzzle. What do you say to that?

"Ro say something," Jared said sitting next to me.

"I think I'm gonna be sick," I said getting up and running to the bathroom. The information was way too much for me.

I should've known that.

After twenty minutes of sitting with my head literally in the toilet I was back in my bed and the others were surrounding my bed. Although it seemed like everything was a complete disaster, I felt content with my circle of friend's right here. They were everything to me even though I still had an open gaping wound in my heart because Dean and Julian said some hurtful and asshole-ish things. I wasn't through from that pain and I knew it.

"So how do we fulfill the prophecy," I said making a small tornado in the water bottle Chad had passed to me.

Julian was making flames hover over his thumb by snapping his fingers. "I don't know," he said not really paying attention to the question.

It was silent for a moment as everyone played absently with their element. Dean was had made a dream catcher with pieces of a tree and vines branch from outside my window. Jared was playing with a water orb that came from the rain outside. Eric was making a small tornado in the air. I want to learn how to do that. Chad, well I really don't know what Chad was doing but his eyes were staring off into space.

"My stomach hurts," I said clutching my stomach. It started hurting right after Dean had told me about the prophecy.

Dean walked out the room for a few minutes and walked back in with a green tea. "Here," he said handing me the cup. "This will make your stomach pains stop. But I warn you that it will make you feel really loopy. It's like a drug of sorts."

I laughed and pushed the tea away from me wincing from the icy pain in my stomach. "I don't do drugs," I whispered.

Dean pushed it back to me with one word. "Drink," he said ending the argument.

I put the cup to my lips and murmured some very rude and ass hat comments. I drank the vile tasting liquid and instantly the pain in my stomach stopped. It was replaced with a fluttery feeling. It calmed me and I felt as though I was floating.

"Stop floating," Eric and Julian said at the same time. Eric had on an amused expression and Julian was scowling at me.

I felt myself return to the bed and I tried to get up. When I got up I fell flat on my face. I heard Eric, Jared and Chad burst into laughter. I started to laugh until I turned over and saw Julian giving me a look that conveyed that he was not at all amused. Dean on the other hand was shaking with suppressed laughter.

Julian took it upon himself to heave me back on the bed. "Stop being goofy," he yelled at me. "We have a problem to deal with."

I covered most of my face with the covers as if I was looking at the boogeyman. "Ohh, scawey," I said in a baby voice. I heard everyone else but Julian giggling. "Sowey," I giggled.

"You're impossible," he yelled in frustration. "Why can't you be serious?"

"Hello I just took some crappy disgusting medicine and it gave me a high," I said stuttering over my words. "Cut me some slack Ju-ju," I said and then covered my mouth because I just said his forbidden nickname. "Oopsie," I murmured.

He turned toward me with a weird look on his face. I really couldn't tell what kind of expression it was because I was completely out of it. "Don't call me that," he said in a whisper.

I went speak but I got dizzy so I put my head back on my pillow. "My head feels funny," I said in a dazed tone.

"The effects of the medicine are working," Dean said walking over and placing his hand on my head. "You will have a slight fever for the next two days so relax when you're in school. Other than that I believe your stomach will be fine."

I started to close my eyes and try to fall asleep but Chad had said something that caught my attention. "What did you say Chad," I asked in a whisper.

"I was just asking what we should do about the Earth demon that is actually our teacher," he said.

"Give him some of that yuck medicine and paint his face when he goes to sleep," I said and laughed. I could just picture his face when he woke up. Black and green symbolizing earth and evil. I would love to see that.

Eric softly laughed and started to get up. "She needs some sleep," he said walking out of the room. "It will soon be day."

"Yea," Chad said following after him. "Night sis."

"Night," I said to all of them as they filed out of my room. "I love my boys," I said before I fell asleep.

Note to self: never drink that awful medicine again. I was having the weirdest dream ever and I think that shit water was the cause.

I was sitting in a room that was much like mine only it was red. There was a beautiful man lying in the bed. He had long black hair and black eyes. I didn't understand his eyes because they changed colors as I moved around him. His skin was unhealthily pale and he looked sick.

There was a woman sitting in the chair next to the bed. She had beautiful blond hair and pale blue eyes. Her skin was a dark tone of amber and her lips were a pretty pale pink. She was gorgeous in every sense of the word.

A young boy walked in the room and I was struck dumbfounded. The boy was a young version of Julian. His short honey brown hair was longer and messier than it is now. His eyes were a dark orange and his skin was not so orange. He was adorable.

"I forgive you," I said.

"I knew this would be harder to do with you and you—wait you forgive me?"

"Yes I forgive you," I laughed. "You have your reasons and I could care less why you were treating me like that. I wouldn't hold a long grudge on you. Julian on the other hand will have to do some major apologies." We both laughed. "You have your moments and I have mine. We still have to get along."

"Thanks," he said pulling me into a hug. "Sorry you missed school but it looked like you were having a good dream," he said opening the door.

"It was an interesting on," I said. "Now if you don't mind I have to see two boys about a bucket of cold water."

"Don't hurt them too bad," he whispered.

I laughed and said, "I won't make any promises."

Later that afternoon, after I used the element of water to drench both Jared and Chad, the boys were sitting in the living room doing their homework. I was in the kitchen making me a sandwich which by the way was the best damn sandwich ever. I was borrowing Chad's iPod so I was listening to Paramore.

"That's what you get when you let your heart win," I was singing and I didn't hear anyone walking up behind me.

"Shit you gave me a fucking heart attack," I said as a soft hand touched my hair. I turned to see Julian looking very sad. "What do you want," I asked as I looked up to him, glaring at him.

He shocked me by pulling me into a hug. I imagine it was the type of hug that the hot werewolf gave the depressed vampire lover in Twilight. This was the same only I'm not depressed nor do I have bad taste in men. I would've picked the guy that was still breathing.

When he let me go I so wanted to laugh because it was such an awkward moment. "What was that for," I asked quietly to maintain composure.

"I need help," he said in a quiet voice.

"With what," I asked out loud. I didn't want to whisper anymore.

He put his hand over my mouth and took my hand. "Follow me," he mouthed.

Who the hell was I to argue seeing that he is easily twice my size and strength? He walked up the stairs and to his room.

When we were in his room he let my hand go and uncovered my mouth. "What the hell are you doing," I asked in frustration.

"I need your help," he said again.

"I got that part," I said louder. "What the hell are we doing in your room?"

When he didn't say anything I started for the door. "Wait," he said sitting on his bed.

I slowly faced him and crossed my arms. "What?"

He rubbed the back of his neck and then ran his fingers through his hair. When he gets vulnerable it's such a turn on. If I was a guy I'd so be sporting wood right now. "What did you say," I asked. While I was visualizing me riding Julian like a cowgirl, he was obviously saying something.

"I want to apologize for everything," he said again quietly. "I said I didn't love you when clearly I can't get you out of my head." He looked at me and I nodded for him to continue. "You frustrate me and turn me on all at the same time. When you give me the cold shoulder is when I love you most." I went to say something but he was too wrapped up in his rambling. "You hold a grudge for 2.2 seconds with everyone else but when it comes to me I just can't get a break with you. You know how to piss me off and then turn around and make me

Everything was trashed. Dishes were broken in the kitchen. The tables and chairs were broken and turned over. The living room was worse. The couches and chairs were torn. The drapes were torn and falling off the wall. The TV was trashed and it was still sparking.

Dean and Jared were laying on the floor all bloody and moaning in pain. The worst thing about it was Chad was there but he wasn't moving. I lied the worst thing about it was the door was open and Eric was gone. How could I say which was worse when they both were gone in some type of way.

"Julian go check if Eric is outside," I yelled running over to Chad. "Chad wake up," I yelled again. When he didn't move I slapped him in the face. "CHAD, DAMN IT OPEN YOUR EYES! PLEASE CHAD PLEASE WAKE UP." This wasn't happening! It couldn't have been happening.

"He's not dead," Dean said coming next to me. "He's been knocked out or put into coma."

Julian came back in the house with Eric limp in his arms and then the water works flew. I cradled Chad to my chest and cried as hard as I could hoping that the life in my boys wouldn't go out. Julian fell to the floor with Eric in his hands and did the same thing that I did.

"We gotta do something," I said between long breathes. "They can't die."

"They won't as long as they are with us," Dean said rubbing my arm trying to give me support. "We have to attack them. They've took enough from us."

I was fighting the anger that was boiling in my chest. "They can't die," I said over and over.

"Use the anger," Julian said quietly. "Dean get away from her." When Dean moved away Julian started talking again. "Let the anger fuel your body so you can bring them back."

I was still fighting to keep my sanity but I was losing. A blue flame engulfed my hands, arms and then my entire body. I let out a scream and I felt myself sanity burst away from me. The dragon in me reared its ugly head in my mind and I knew the monster was back again.

When Chad started breathing in my arms I stopped screaming. "Ro," he whispered, voice broken and shattered.

I hugged him closer to me and whispered back. "I'm here baby. I'm right here." I rocked him back and forth.

I heard Eric start breathing and looked over to see Julian hugging his brother.

"When we go to school tomorrow," I started. "I will kill that brutal vile creature." My voice wasn't even recognizable to me. The old quiet Roel has left the building.

I woke up the next morning to a creepily quiet house. I went to the bathroom and looked in the mirror. My eyes had spots of black white and gray. They looked scary from all angles. My hair was a deeper color black if it could get any darker. When I turned my head there were deep purple streaks through my hair.

I took a shower and went to cook breakfast. The house was so quiet but so tense. I looked over my shoulder every step I took. The kitchen was worse. Julian and Jared sat tensed in the stools by the island. Dean was leaning on the counter looking absently out the window.

"How are they," I whispered causing them to tense a bit more. "Sorry for scaring you."

"They're fine," Dean whispered. "They are sleeping in the same room. I'll stay home with them."

"I'll stay too," I said rummaging through the fridge to find some bacon and eggs.

"No you need to go to school," he argued. I turned to protest but he started talking again. "What happen to your eyes?"

I turned back to the fridge and closed it. "I don't know," I said. "They were like this when I woke up this morning."

He took my face in his hands and looked closer into my eyes. "You do have all the elements. You must have come to you full powers last night."

I had started cooking the eggs and bacon. I didn't want to talk about last night because I was surely going to burst if I thought about it.

"I'm going to get ready for school," I said trying to control my anger. I ran upstairs and slammed my door.

I could feel my body heating up but I couldn't let my anger get the best of me right now. I got dressed and went back downstairs. I decided that since I'm going to kill a soul sucking demon today I would wear and t-shirt and some jeans. The t-shirt had a heart with a spear through, blood was splattered all over the shirt and the spear was on fire. I'm on a mission and I intend to fulfill it.

When I went downstairs Julian was sitting at the bottom of the stairs waiting for me. "You going to school with me," I asked.

"I have to keep someone safe," he said with a humorless laugh. "We're waiting on Jared." He looked to the door with a blank face. "I didn't know what to do you know," he said randomly.

"What do you mean," I asked skeptically.

"I thought he was going to die," he said. "Not this time but when I lost control the last time. I thought he was dead and it was my fault. Then this happens and I couldn't stop it because—because," he started to cry and I felt his agony. I felt the same way.

I took his head and placed it on my chest, where my heart beats. "You helped me save him this time," I whispered. "They are alive and breathing. We will get these bitch ass demons back for this." When he stopped sobbing I took his face in my hands. "We'll do this together. I, you and Jared will get this asshole."

He nodded and hugged me again. He was so shaken and I didn't want to see him like that ever again.

When Jared came downstairs it was a sad, sad moment. He wasn't his goofy happy self anymore and it pained my heart.

"You alright, Jared," I asked pulling him into a hug. I didn't want to let him go because he felt too warm to my cold air.

"I'm fine, my precious," he said putting on his best smile but it didn't reach his eyes. "You look totally ready to kick someone's ass right now."

I laughed and said, "I feel ready to kick someone's ass right now." We walked out the door and the sky was gray, no clouds just gray. It was like all the happiness was gone to the world. I felt the tension grow stronger as we walked to school.

I almost lost my temper when we reached the school grounds. "Cool it Ro," Julian said. "Your hair is flaming up."

I closed my eyes and cooled down internally. "Sorry," I murmured under my breath.

When I walked Julian to his first class Julia rudely interrupted us. The bitch was stupid to mess with me today.

"Look what the cat dragged in," she said to her Barbie dolls that were behind her. "Julian what did I tell you about hanging with the help?"

I threw her into a locker and got in her face. "Listen whore-bag, I've had a long night and you're pissing me off. I would advise you to stay clear of me, Julian and Jared today or your pretty porcelain face will be on a stick with your pretty wannabes behind it." She looked shocked and even scared. "Fuck off," I said throwing her in the classroom.

"That was hot," Julian whispered behind me. I turned to him giving him a non-amused face. "Sorry," he murmured. "I'll see you at lunch."

"Okay," I said and walked off. I went to get my homework from the non-immortal teachers and resided in the library to do my work.

Before I knew it two hours had passed by. We had lunch in an hour so I decided to take some time off the work. I put on my iPod and started reading this House of Night book 4.

I was so into my reading that I didn't notice the hot guy in front of me. He was tall and lean. His eyes were like Julian's only they were darker. His hair was shoulder length and a pretty bronze color and his skin was a creamy peach color.

"What," I asked after I took out my headphones. That's when it hit me. His eyes were like Julian's. Julian's eyes were orange because he had the element of fire. This mysterious creature had to be a demon. So why didn't I get that uneasy eerie feeling?

"You're Chad's sister am I correct," he said with unexpected properness.

"It depends on whose asking," I said skeptically. "What or who are you?"

"My name is Blake," he said in that unexpected tone again. "And I am a fire demon. But I didn't come here to hurt you or anything."

"That's the first," I laughed sarcastically. "You actually came to talk to me?"

"Well my fellow brothers told me about the angry Blackness they sent to your home and they told me they almost killed two of you," he said.

I felt my eyes flame and I closed them quickly. "Don't remind me," I said in a calm yet controlled tone. "So what do you want from Chad?"

"There is a reason why I don't roll with my brothers," he gestured to the chair, "may I sit?" I nodded and he sat and continued. "Chad is like my best friend. I know he's gay and I know you're his sister. I don't like what my brothers do because it's taking control of them and they're not quite themselves. The Blackness that invaded your house has corrupted them in more ways than one. We are considered the Evil to our half dragon cousins and we live with it. Yet my brothers are being possessed by another kind of evil. We have to live together on terms and they are being broken.

"With that said I wanted to let you know that I'm kind of on your side with this. I'm willing to eliminate my brothers and what it is that they are embracing."

I didn't know what to say because I was still processing the thoughts in my head. Finally I found the words and said, "How do I know I can trust you?"

"You don't," he said simply. "But you can give me a chance and see that I am not at all like my brothers."

I contemplated the thought before I said, "Well your green eyed earth wielding brother will be the first to go. And he's going today."

"As long as I can help you take him down," he said smugly.

"I'll take you up on that offer."

Walking to lunch, Blake and I both talked about how we could kill or badly hurt his big brother, whose name is Blair. We had got to our outside spot before Julian but Jared was there.

"Hey, Blake," Jared sang. "How are you?"

"Not in the greatest of moods," Blake said with a ghost smile. "Do you know how Chad's doing?"

Jared sadly shook his head. In that same moment Julian came walking casually over. He tensed when he was Blake sitting next to me.

"Blake," Julian said coldly. "Still trying to claim your innocence I see."

"You know that I'm not like them Julian," he argued. "I'm merely evil by association."

"Keep telling yourself that, Flames," Julian shot back sitting down on the other side of me. He turned his attention on me and pulled my face up with his finger. He looked deeply into my eye and said, "You have pretty eyes."

I blushed deeply and took his hand from my face and smiled. "Since when did my eyes become the importance at hand?"

"Since your little burst of power last night," he said kissing my cheek. He was back to the boy I knew and fell in love with.

"Well let's not think about my eyes at this moment," I said pulling myself from his distraction. "Blake and I have been talking about how to go about Blair."

"Who the hell is Blair," both Julian and Jared asked.

"Earth demon," I said, "keep up. We need to get him alone and away from the mortals which will be exceedingly hard seeing that he teaches class."

"Why can't we do it after school," Julian asked finally on board that we have Blake as an asset. "Wouldn't it better if he was cornered or something?"

"That's sound plausible," Blake said. "How would he fall for something like that?"

"Bait," I said looking at Blake mischievously.

"You're not using me as bait," he defended. When I didn't look away he murmured some unholy remarks under his breath. "Fine," he said. "You better kill him too."

I laughed wickedly and said, "I plan to."

Chapter 8

Before lunch had ended I decided that I was going to go to art today. It was a way of saying that I'm not afraid of anything and the fact that this soul sucker tried to kill my brother and my best friend is angering me to different levels.

When I walked into the room I felt the uneasy eerie feeling. There was something wrong with this feeling though. It was getting worse as I went to my seat. That's when I realized the white headed demon sitting down with, guess who, the ever so lovely Julia.

"Bro," the white headed demon said to Blake. "Since when did you start rolling with the good guys?"

"Shove it Byron," Blake said through clenched teeth. He was getting ready to hit his brother but I held him back. "You tried to kill my best friend. I should rip your freaking head off."

"Not here, Blake," I whispered. "Not now."

"So you have a stray," Byron said. "And who is this pretty young thing?" Before I could answer something went off in his head and his eyes lit up. "Ahh . . . You must be the infamous Roel," he said looking deep into my eyes. His eyes were blue and silver. He must have the element air or spirit. "You do wield all the elements. You're eyes tell it all."

"Bite me, asshole," I said to him with a wicked smile.

110

"Smart mouth," he said with the same wicked smile. "You know that your mouth will well enough get you killed."

"I'm hoping it will be the other way around," I said with too much wickedness in my voice.

"Enough," I heard someone say from behind me. I turned to see the shitty green eyed demon glaring at me. "Class, please take your seats." His glare turned into an almost friendly stare. "Roel, it's nice of you to grace us with your presents again. I assume you won't be walking out today?"

I still glared at him and he laughed mockingly. "I'm don't plan on it Blair, I mean Mr. Lee," I said in a mocking tone.

His face turned pale for a split second. "Well class you have your assignment. It should be done by the end of class." He turned to his white headed brother and said. "Byron, will you be so kind to fill Roel and Julia on what we need to do today?"

"Sure Mr. Lee," he said smiling wickedly again. He walked over to me and I tried to hold myself together.

"I'll help her," Julian said stepping between us. "You help the skag-bag over there," he pointed over to Julia on the other side of the room.

While Julian filled me in on the info for class Julia murmured some very derogatory remarks under her breath. It was getting harder to work with the plan now that Byron was a part of it.

"How are we going to do this now," I whispered to Julian and Blake.

"I don't know," Blake said. "What about your brother, Jared," he asked Julian. "Can he find a way here to help?"

"Mr. Lee," I called out. "May I use the bathroom?"

"Have you started your painting," he asked.

"Yes," I said rolling my eyes acting as if I really had to go.

"Then you may go," he said surprisingly. "Hurry back," he added.

"Ok," I said. I turned to Julian and whispered, "Where is Jared right now?"

"Down the hall," he said. "By our lockers."

I started for the door until I heard, "I have to go too." Byron was the voice behind the comment.

I darted down the hall toward Jared's room and wave him down through the window. He was giving me a weird look so I kept waving at him frantically. When he finally came out of the classroom took his hand and ran further down the hall.

"We have problems," I said through heavy breathing. "Blake's brother, Byron is here."

"Shit the spirit demon," he said. "We need to get to a safer place to talk." He ran further down the hall until we got to the girls bathroom. When we got there he closed his eyes and went in.

"Why the hell are we in here," I asked.

He laughed and said, "What guy, especially a demon, would in their right mind come into a girl's bathroom without a girl? Now if someone comes in here pretend we're making out or something."

I laughed and said, "Back to the situation that is getting more and more complicated, we have to do something about the other demon."

"Well what can we do," he asked his eyes still closed.

"You can open your eyes. It's only us in here," I said with a humorous tone.

When he opened his eyes he smiled at me and said, "You really do have pretty eyes." When I blushed he kissed me on the cheek. "You get as red as a tomato when you blush. From now on I'll call you Rosy Red."

"Would you stop being so goofy and help me figure out what we're gonna do," I said pushing him away slightly.

"Well we can kill him when we kill the earth demon, Blair right," he said and I nodded. "How can we do that?"

"It will be the four of us against the two of them," I said. "It shouldn't be that hard. We have all five elements on our side and plus you guys hold each element." I tapped my lip with my fingers and thought for a moment. "What about Julia? I think she's gonna help them." I leaned on the sink and thought some more.

He leaned on the stall door and put on the same puzzled look I had. "I don't know," he said. "Maybe we can get rid of her before we try to go after the demons."

I started getting fidgety thinking that we might not be able to pull this off. "I'll think of something while I'm in class. We'd better go before people come looking for us."

"Yea we'd better," he said walking out the door behind me. I came to a complete stop when the uneasy feeling hit me. "Roel what the-"

I put my hand up to stop him. "One of them is in the hallway," I whispered. I looked down the hall but I didn't see anyone. I looked the other way to find the white headed demon looking dead at us.

"Clever that you can figure out when a demon is present," he said in an eerie tone. "It will come in handy when you are about to die. It won't be a surprise."

"I'll kill you first, suck-bag," I said through clenched teeth. "You tried to kill my brothers and for that you will die."

His skin twitched and started to crawl. "I beg to differ, my sweet," he said in an unrecognizable voice. The voice was creepy and very scary. It was like something out of the Exorcist. "You will feel the wrath of my Blackness soon enough." When his skin stopped twitching he said in his normal voice. "You will die before us. Even if we have to take them entire half dragon race down with you." He walked away.

Before he could get any further I felt myself burst with energy. My hair was on fire and my eyes were flaming blue. My hands glowed with blue, red and silver flames. I threw the balls of fire toward him and he went up in flames. "Dare threaten my family again and I will make sure these flames kill you," I said in a wicked tone. When the flames on him went out I walked over to find him still breathing. "You can threaten me all you like but when you threaten Dean, Jared, Julian, Eric, and Chad it's a problem.

"That was a warning shot. Do something stupid again and I will make sure my elements turn their backs on each and every one of you suck-heads and drown you in your own powers." I bent down in his face and said, "Do I make myself clear?"

With eyes wide and mouth ajar he nodded. I kept my glare on him unto he turned away.

I put on my best wicked smile and said, "Good because I won't make the next shot that sweet." I got up and walked down the hall leaving the demon to wallow in his pain and tears.

Jared pulled me to a stop when we reached his room. "That was totally hot," he said. "You should lose your temper more often." When I turned to him he jumped back. "Girl your eyes just keep getting weirder."

I blinked and rubbed my eyes. "What's wrong with them," I asked.

"They have red and orange in them now," he said taking my head in his hands. "They look cool though."

"Great," I said throwing my hands up. "Now I have weird eyes."

He started to laugh. "Your eyes look fine," he said taking my hands in his. "Now go back to class and tell Julian how you almost fried the white headed soul sucker."

I gave him a childish, "Okay," and went back to class. When I returned I gave Blair, Mr. Lee a wicked smirk. "Back," I said smugly.

When I sat next to Julian he gave me a skeptical look. "What the hell happened," he whispered. When I turned to tell him what happened, his eyes went wide. "Roel what did you do now?"

"I almost fried the white haired suck-head," I said with confidence. "He threatened my family so I threw flames at him." I got closer to him. "And then I got these cool red and orange specks in my eyes. See," I opened my eyes wide so he can see.

"You are something else Ro," he laughed. "But your eyes do look hotter."

"Well thank you," I said and went back to painting. "We shouldn't have to worry about this other demon though. I believe he will head this warning."

When Byron walked back in the room I knew I was right. Even though he didn't have any burns the agony was written on his face. He was in extra pain and I was happy that I caused it. Maybe now they'll learn not to mess with me and my family. Maybe they'll leave us alone and stop the madness so we can live in peace. Maybe this world of peace I'm dreaming of will become reality. HA who the hell am I kidding?

Byron went back to sit in his seat and I smiled wickedly at him.

You know I can read you mind, a voice hand in my head. I turned to Mr. Lee and smiled.

You can, I asked and he nodded. *Good then listen closely. I'm about two seconds away from frying the both of you.* I thought about taking the air from his lungs and at that moment he started choking. *I can kill each of you in more ways than one. Read my thoughts on what I said to your brother and remember that it goes for you too. Touch my family again and I will make sure you are buried with your own element. If you don't head my warning I will kill you slowly and painfully. Am I clear?* He nodded and I let the air back in his lungs. He started coughing and I glared at him.

The secretary walked the room and handed Blair a note. He read it and said "Julian and Roel, you are free to go."

I looked at him with a confused expression. He rolled his eyes and said, "Dean is here to pick you guys up."

We gathered our things and headed for the door. I looked toward Blake and gave him a sad smile and waved. I looked between Blair and Byron and flipped them off. *Cool flipping off a teacher, Ro,* I thought to myself. I didn't care. He wasn't a teacher to me.

We walked to office to find Dean and Chad at the door. When I saw Chad I felt my heart stop. He was really here and alive. "CHAD," I yelled and ran to him. I jumped in his arms and he twirled me around. I felt the tears flow down my cheeks and I squeezed my eyes shut. "I love you bro," I whispered.

"I love you too Ro," he whispered back. When he put me down I realized he was crying.

I wiped my tears and said, "Where's Eric?"

"He's home and he's fine," Dean said. "We have problems though so I need you guys back home. We'll be out for the next few days so we need to pack."

"What's wrong," I asked but I was cut short.

"Uncle's coming isn't he," Julian asked. "He's coming without mom."

"Yes and we'll talk about it later," Dean said and walked out of the office. We all followed and found Jared outside waiting.

"Can we hurry this up please," he said jumping in place.

We all ran home and hoped that we didn't run into their father. It was hard to avoid their uncle due to the fact that he was already in the driveway.

"Shit," they all muttered under their breaths.

"I assume this will not go well," I said as we walked through the door.

"Not at all," Julian said under his breath.

"Great," I said under my breath. As I walked in the living room I thought I looked into a mirror. The only difference was that this was a man.

He had shoulder length black hair like mine and piercing blue eyes. He was tall and muscular just like Chad. His skin was darker than mine but it didn't matter. He was my twin in every sense of the word.

"Who the hell is she," he asked his voice booming across the house.

"Who wants to know," I defended. "Who the hell are you?"

"I'm their uncle," he said crossing his arms. "Now I ask again, who the hell are you?"

"I'm their sister," I said giving him the same closed off expression. "Let's not do this whole sing and dance because you won't win." I glared at him and he did the same.

"This isn't gonna end well," Chad said sitting down on the couch. Everyone followed him and sat around us.

I wasn't giving up and I had a feeling neither was he. In this month I've been through too much just to let some asshole old guy scare me. I've made it clear that I am now the big bitch around here and I demand respect. And the showdown continues.

Finally after about twenty minutes of glaring at each other he turned away. Nobody scares Roel.

"My name is Cameron," he said finally. "And you are," he asked.

"Roel," I said. He looked at Julian and I snapped my fingers in his face. "That's not important at the moment. Why the hell are you here?"

"Well clearly these boys need some help on what they bring in this house," he said sitting down. "I'm their uncle and what I say goes."

I laughed condescendingly. "Were you helping when they were fighting for their lives yesterday? Or when they were in school with shit headed demons? Or when that shitty Blackness tried to consume my brother and my best friend? Or when a demon entered this house trying to kill us? Hell, no you wasn't there," I said with no recognition of who I was talking to or what I was saying. "You were some other place and I was there to save them. I brought Eric and Chad back to life so who the hell are you to say about what they bring in this house? I have fought for them ever since I walked through that door and I won't stop fighting for them until I breathe my last breath."

I could feel the shocked stares from everyone in the room. They were as shocked as I was. Where that came from I don't know but I'm done with people talking down to me.

Then Cameron laughed sarcastically. "So you're the reason Eric and Chad are alive?" he stood and sized me up. "I was hoping you'd be much classier looking. You are no threat to the demons you're up against. You've been truly mistaken if you think you can hold your own in a battle. You've been given powers that are far beyond you." He walked past me and toward the kitchen. "Like I said boys I know what's best for you and she isn't it. She needs to go."

"Uncle Cam," Dean said getting up from the couch when I didn't make a move.

I was stuck in place and I hardly heard the conversation and uproar that was going on around me. *He said you're inferior to them,* a voice said in my head.

Shut up, I thought back. *I'm better than to let that stop be from being who I am.*

You're not shit is what he's telling you!

But I know better now get the fuck out of my head.

I shook the voice off physically and mentally and came back to the real world. Julian and Dean were shouting at the tops of their lungs at their uncle and Jared, Chad and Eric were fuming.

"Listen," I said but no one heard me. "Hey," I said louder getting the attention from the three that weren't about to go for World War 3.

Out of sheer annoyance of being ignored I cut the air supply off from the arguing men, "Will you guys just shut the hell up?" I gave them back their air as they fell to the ground.

"Are you guys done with your bitching," I asked. When they nodded their agreement I continued. "Good now listen. Uncle Cam or whoever you are I want to let you know that it will take a lot more than some wigged out pig headed adult to get me out of this house. Unless the five of them have a problem with it then I'm not going anywhere. And for the two of you," I pointed to Julian and Dean who were still heavy breathing. "You two of all people should know that when it comes to arguments that I can hold my own. No need to worry about me as of this moment. If it isn't the demons that have been allying with Blackness then don't run unless I call.

"Back to you, ass hat," I turned back to Cameron and started walking toward him. "You've got the nerve to come here and call me inferior."

"I didn't-"

"Shut the hell up I'm not done yet," I snapped slamming him into a wall with a burst of air. "You haven't a clue what the hell I've been through the last few weeks. I've been hit in the head, scared to death, passed or three or four times, became a demon dragon or angel dragon, I've had poison ivy in all the wrong places, threatened by the entire snake demon race and on top of all of that I am destined to be the one that will help the balance of good and evil be restored. If you think I can't handle it then you be my guest." I flamed up and finished my speech.

"If you haven't noticed I'm equipped with each of the elements and some other funky shit that I have yet to figure out. From the color of your eyes I believe you can control water. If I'm not fully equipped for this war then by all means dare try to do it better. From the looks of it you won't be able to do any better than what I've already done." I de-flamed and stuck my hand out to help him up.

"Does she regularly go off like this," Cameron said not taking his eyes off me. "Damn she reminds me of your mom."

"She's been getting more and more ticked off lately," Julian said pulling me to him. "She has a short temper meter."

"I've noticed," he said still looking at me. It was a look of awe and respect. I was finding it more and more relaxing. "Sorry to upset you, gorgeous," my said kissing my hand.

"Back off Cam," Jared and Julian said and I laughed. These boys are gonna have a heart attack over me.

"What the hell are you doing here anyway Uncle Cam," Chad asked.

"As I told you before rainbow balls," he said giving Chad a sideways look. "I'm not you fucking uncle. I still can't believe their mom took you in."

My eyes flamed and I constricted his air again. "Don't talk to my brother like that shit for brains."

"Okay, okay I'm sorry," he said choking on his words. I let go of him mentally and he fell on the floor. "Jeez Julian tame your shrew," he said through heavy breathing.

Julian laughed and pulled me into a hug. "I'm sorry uncle but this feisty dragon that I fell in love with just can't be tamed," he said and kissed me.

And in that moment the world didn't matter. No one else but this orange god mattered.

Chapter 9

Chad and I were sitting in his room looking up at the ceiling. "What the hell is up with everyone hating you and the fact that you're gay," I asked randomly. "I love you like that."

He laughed and said, "Well how would you feel if your room looked the sun and the rest of the house looks like something out of the medieval times? Plus I'm a ray of fucking sunshine and they are pessimists."

"Sometimes that scares me about you," I said turning over to look at him. "You scared the hell out of me you know that? It was hard to be strong. I can't do that again."

Pulled my head to his chest and stroked my hair. "I'm sorry I scared you, muffin," he said into my hair. "Thank you for saving me, too. I thought I was gone for good." He was back to his happy self and it scared me.

"Dude snap out of it," I said snapping my fingers in his face. "Chad you died and I had to bring you back." I got up from the floor and stood over him as he sat up. "You don't know the feeling of hurt when you feel something is wrong. You and Eric were almost really gone. You can actually sit here and be happy about it?"

"That's all I have," he argued. "I've been talked about, teased, beat up and hurt by everyone that I have to be happy with what happens to me. What if I did die last night? Everyone in this house would be so sad and angry. It would be like the happiness was gone from the house. I bring out their happiness by being me."

"But you don't have to be happy about dying," I said with tears. "It's not something any of us should be facing right now. I'm strong enough to make threats and scare the living shit out of some Blackness binding demon. I'm not strong enough to lose one of you." I sat on the bed and folded my arms across my body. "I almost passed the hell out when I saw you and when Julian walked back in the house with a lifeless Eric. I don't know if you know what it feels like to see a person you love dead. I don't want to see it again."

He sat next to me and pulled me into him. "Muffin, I'm sorry. I didn't think you'd be upset if I was back to myself. I didn't want to be all suck head and sad because I almost lost my life. I knew you would save me." He put his hand under my chin and raised my head to look at him. "You are as strong as I thought you were and you fixed everything. You're strong enough to make a race of suck head demons disappear. You're hot and all kinds of powerful."

I laughed and did the sniffle song. "Thank you for making me feel better," I said.

"Anything for my Ro," he said kissing the top of my head. "Oh my Dean didn't lie. You're eyes are pretty. They suit you very well. He didn't tell me about the orange and red though."

"That happened in school," I said smiling in confidence. "A spirit demon decided that he wanted to try and threaten you guys so I had to fix that."

"Cool," he said. "I'm hungry. We should go get something to eat."

"That sounds fun," I said walking to the door with my brother in hand.

We went downstairs to find Dean and Cameron fighting. They had destroyed the living room and were tempting to ruin the clean white kitchen.

"Hey," I yelled at my hair burst into bright blue flames. "What the hell?!"

They both stopped and looked at me. A mixture of awe and confusion filled their faces and the faces of the boys watching the fight.

"This is a whole other form of idiocy," I yelled. "You don't clean this house. I do. Dean you should be the smartest out of the two of you."

"But-"

"But what Dean," I yelled. "You know I clean this freaking house so why the hell would you get into a pointless fight."

"He's trying to kick you and Chad out," Dean yelled. "I had to stop him and Julian from fighting and he hit me," he pointed to Cameron.

I turned to Cameron and glared at him wickedly. "How many times do I have to tell you that I'm not going anywhere? And then you try to put my brother out on the street? You son of a bitch. I will not stand for this."

"Nor will I," said a voice from the door. A glaring Goddess was looking at Cameron with wicked eyes. Her eyes were pale blue and her hair was a pretty blond. She had bright pink lips like Jared but she was as tall as Eric. Now I know who this is. It's their mom.

"Amanda," Cameron stuttered. "What, what are you doing here?"

"Obviously saving my son and this beauty from you beasty ass," she snipped. "How dare you defy me and my decisions about who I bring to this house? You should be ashamed."

"I'm sorry," he said and bowed his head to her. That was a sign of respect I didn't see coming.

"Now what is your name," she said walking up to me.

"Roel," I said absently. I was still struck by the fact that I was staring at their mom. She was amazingly beautiful.

"Well, Roel, it is a pleasure to meet you," she stretched out her hand and I shook it.

"Enchanter," I said back. "I'm sorry if I'm staring but I've heard a lot about you and I can't believe I'm actually meeting you."

She laughed and said, "Roel you talk as if I'm some kind of celebrity. I'm just their mom."

"And they were right about you," I said. "You are so pretty."

"Likewise, my darling," she said touching my hair. "Your hair is as dark as a raven's wings. It's fascinating."

"Thank you," I said putting on my best smile.

"Mom," said the five angels behind her. They all ran to her and hugged her.

"Hey sweeties," she said to all of them. She kissed their heads and tousled their hair. "How have you guys been?"

Murmurs of groans and heavy sighs filled the room. "We've been in agony," Julian said.

"What's wrong," she said her eyebrow pulling together causing wrinkles to flood her seamless face.

"Demons," Eric said. I forgot he was in the room until he spoke from behind me.

"Ass hat, soul sucking demons," I murmured. "I hate those sons of bitches."

"I assure you that you are not the only one," she said. "They are certainly the evil red headed step children of our kinds." We all laughed.

"What are you doing here mom," Dean asked looking like a little kid.

"Well I've been having weird feelings about you guys," she said. "You've been having issues with these demons as you said but something about it isn't right."

"Like the fact that they are being possessed by Blackness," I mumbled.

"What did you say," she said her head snapping toward me.

"Some of them are being possessed by this thing called Blackness," I said. "One of them, Blake, said that he doesn't like the way his brothers have been acting."

"So are they trying to kill you guys," she asked.

"When are they not," Chad said. "We've been trying to get rid of them but we can't do it alone. This blue eyed beauty here," he put his arms around me, "has been scaring the shit out of these fuckers for a couple of days."

"You should've seen her today," Jared said putting his arm over my shoulder. "She almost burned one to a crisp. Then she threatened him and put so much fear in him I thought he was gonna shit him."

"Well I see that you guys are well taken care of," she said looking a little sad. "So do you guys no longer need me?"

"Mom don't think like that," Dean said hugging her. "We need more than you know it. We've missed you."

They all hovered around their mom and I felt almost out of place. They were all happy and their faces were alight. I will never get the chance to see my mom again. I don't even know where she is. And to see them like this, it makes me want to cry. I may be strong but this is a weakness I cannot face.

I retreated to my room slowly and realized that if their mom is staying then she might want her room back. After I closed the door I let the tears fall from my eyes. I'll be stronger another time.

I don't know how long I leaned on my door silently crying but I knew that several times someone knocked on the door.

"Who is it," I sniffled.

"It's me," a booming voice said from the other side of the door.

"What do you want," I said sniffling again.

"Open the door Ro," he said.

I got up from the floor and opened the door. I stood there looking at the orange beauty for a while before walking over to my bed.

"Why are you crying," he said sitting next to me on my bed.

"What shouldn't I be crying," I said. "You guys have your mother back. I can tell that she's gonna stay so you guys don't need me."

He pulled into his chest and stroked my hair. "Hey, hey don't think like that," he whispered. "She's not staying with us. She doesn't even want to stay." I looked up at him furrowing my eyebrows. "We asked her why and she said we don't need her as much as we think we do."

"But you—I mean—the way you lit up when you saw her. I can't compete with that."

"You don't have to," he said kissing my forehead. "She wants you to stay and wants you to help us." I gave him another blank face. "Roel you changed us big time. You brought happiness back into this house when there was nothing but pain and despair. She said she feels that happiness in us today."

What do you say to that? "I'm not going anywhere," was all I could say.

"So what else is eating at you," he said pulling me down to the bed.

"The way she looks at you guys with so much love and caring," I said messing with a lock of my hair. "She's your mom, you know. She gives off that motherly vibe when she's around you guys. I don't have anyone to look at me like that." And there goes the waterworks. "Chad even had someone to replace her, you know. I don't have anyone to call mom. I don't know where she is and what she looks like."

It was his turn to be speechless. What could he say? "We could help you find her," he whispered.

That stopped the crying and sniffling for a heartbeat of a moment. "What did you say," I said through a shaky voice.

"The boys and I will help you find her," he said a little louder. "Plus it would make Chad happier if he found his real mom."

"You mean it," I asked not falling on false hope just yet.

"I promise, Roel Zoey Summers, that I, Julian White, will do whatever it is in my power to help you find your mother."

"Promise," I asked again.

"Promise."

Chapter 10

A Month Into School

"Remind me to kill Julian and Chad," I told Eric and he laughed. I punched him in the arm lightly and said, "I'm so serious."

"You can't be mad at them," he said putting his arm over my shoulder. "You know for sure that this was the right thing to do."

"Because he's Julian and I'm Roel," I said. "We have to play as Romeo and Juliet."

"Yes," he said simply. "That's exactly why you two have to play the roles"

"This sucks," I said. We're sitting in the drama room when Julian and Chad walked in. "You two need to go away," I said glaring at them.

"What's wrong sis," Chad said coming over to hug me.

"I can't act, that's what's wrong," I said pushing away from him. "I don't like plays."

"Neither do I, babe," Julian said grabbing me from behind. "The teacher thought that since we are here that we should play the part."

"I can't believe you are making me audition for this crap," I said leaning my head back on his shoulders. "You suck big time for this."

"Julian and Roel," the drama teacher called out, "playing for the parts of Romeo and Juliet."

"Great," I groaned and took the stage.

"We will be doing Act I Scene V where Romeo first meets Juliet," Drama Teacher said. "Eric will play Benvolio. Chad will play Capulet. I will say the words of the nurse. And Action," she yelled.

Here goes nothing.

ROMEO [*To JULIET.*]
If I profane with my unworthiest hand
 This holy shrine, the gentle sin is this:
 My lips, two blushing pilgrims, ready stand
To smooth that rough touch with a tender kiss.
JULIET
Good pilgrim, you do wrong your hand too much,
 Which mannerly devotion shows in this;
 For saints have hands that pilgrims' hands do touch, And palm to palm is holy palmers' kiss.
ROMEO
Have not saints lips, and holy palmers too?
JULIET
Ay, pilgrim, lips that they must use in prayer.
ROMEO
O, then, dear saint, let lips do what hands do;
They pray — grant thou, lest faith turn to despair.
JULIET
Saints do not move, though grant for prayers' sake.
ROMEO
Then move not, while my prayer's effect I take.
[*Kisses her.*]
Thus from my lips, by yours, my sin is purged.

JULIET
Then have my lips the sin that they have took.
ROMEO
Sin from thy lips? O trespass sweetly urged!
110 Give me my sin again.
[Kisses her.]
JULIET
You kiss by th' book.
Nurse *[Suddenly appearing.]*
Madam, your mother craves a word with you.
[Juliet moves away.]
ROMEO
What is her mother?
Nurse
 Marry, bachelor,
 Her mother is the lady of the house,
 And a good lady, and a wise and virtuous
 I nursed her daughter, that you talk'd withal;
 I tell you, he that can lay hold of her
 Shall have the chinks.
[The Nurse goes after Juliet.]
ROMEO
 Is she a Capulet?
 O dear account! my life is my foe's debt.
BENVOLIO *[Suddenly appearing.]*
 Away, begone; the sport is at the best.
ROMEO
 Ay, so I fear; the more is my unrest.
CAPULET
Nay, gentlemen, prepare not to be gone;
We have a trifling foolish banquet towards.
Is it e'en so? why, then, I thank you all
I thank you, honest gentlemen; good night.
 More torches here! Come on then, let's to bed.
 Ah, sirrah, by my fay, it waxes late:
 I'll to my rest.

To my surprise the crowd that was watching gave us all a standing ovation. Note so self: remember to kill Julian and Chad for this.

"That was beyond amazement," the drama teacher said with tears in her eyes. "You all are talented beyond words."

"So are you telling me we got the parts," I asked her. When she nodded I groaned and sulked all the way to my seat.

"You'll do fine Ro," Julian said putting his arm around me and kissing the side of me. "I'm here right with you."

"That helps," I said sarcastically. "You're just gonna make a fool of yourself with me."

"When you put it like that, I would love to make a fool of myself with you." He went for a kiss on the lips and I turned my head.

"Julian, not right now," I said turning back to him. "I'm not ready for that again."

Things haven't been really physical with me and Julian ever since Chad and Eric got hurt. I want to kiss him but I can't bring myself to do it again.

"I know Roel I just forgot," he said kissing the side of my head. "I'm sorry."

"It's fine," I told him truthfully.

Dean and is freaky looking girlfriend walked in. Elizabeth was a tall chick with blonde hair and piercing blue eyes. She had pale skin but I guess it fit her. I didn't like her very much but I never told anyone. She was suspiciously awkward and she was rude to me when the boys weren't around.

"Hi, guys," Dean chimed. He was extra happy today and I didn't like that.

"Hey, Dean," I said with false enthusiasm. He didn't notice or I think he just didn't care. I could actually care less if he cares because the only girl that's important to him now is his scary looking girlfriend.

"Hey Jewel, what's wrong," Dean asked putting his arm around me.

"Having a rough day," I said looking away from him. "Sort of like you girlfriend with her hair.

"Roel you don't have to be rude," Dean said punching me lightly in my arm. "What's with you?"

"She's just having trust issues," Elizabeth said. "I don't mind that."

"That's not true is it Ro," Dean asked me with pleading eyes.

I wanted to say that it wasn't true but something about her was just way off. "Sorry Dean but your little girlfriend is right, I don't trust her and you shouldn't trust her either." I got up and walked out and Dean followed me into the hallway.

"Wait, Roel, why don't you like her," he asked almost hurt.

"I don't know Dean," I said throwing my hands up. "I just have a feeling about her."

"That doesn't mean you can just be mean to her," he said crossing his arms over his chest and leaning against the wall. "You can at least try to get along with her."

"I tried that when I first met her," I said mimicking his actions. "She's evil."

He laughed and looked at me. "She's not evil. She's sweet and kind."

"She hangs out with that demon," I yelled. "She has something to do with that Blackness. I know she does."

At that moment the evil queen walked out the door. "Sweetie, go back inside with your brother I'll talk to Roel."

"Actually I'll go back inside," I said but Dean stopped me.

"No," he said with a straight face. "Stay out here and talk with her, please."

I hate when he says 'please'. "Fine," I said and leaned back on the wall.

When Dean walked back in the drama room Elizabeth turned to me with blackness in her eyes. "You little bitch," she said in a menacing voice. Her eyes changed back to normal and she looked less crazy.

"I knew it," I said casually on the wall. "I knew you were a part of that whole evil Blackness takeover. You never fooled me. So, which one turned you?"

"Byron," she said leaning on the wall next to me. "He told me and my good friend Julia that the Blackness can get you anything you want. He was right. I got Dean and he thinks I'm a fucking princess. Little does he know I'm corrupting him and when he's fully into me, I'll give him what he wants."

"Over my dead body," I said my eyes flaming up. "You hurt Dean-"

"You've mistaken, Roel," she said with those black eyes again. "I'm not here to hurt Dean. I'm here to turn him, make him one of us."

"And I say again cunt sucker," I said taking the air away from her making her fall to her knees, "over my dead body. See, I have the ability to kill all of you and I hold back because we are in a place full of mortals. So when the time is right I'll make sure you fuck faces feel the wrath of my anger." I gave her back her air and walked back into the drama room.

"So are you guys good," Dean asked with a disgusted admiring look on his face. This bitch really has a hold on my brother. I'll let it go for now but if he makes me do some shit like this again I'll burn him.

"We've come to an agreement," I said as she walked into the room. "I knew I was right but I'll let you find out on your own. Until then I have nothing to say about her or you."

"Wait," he said grabbing my arm. "What does that mean?"

"It means she's still not trusted," I said tugging my arm away from his grip. "And as long as you date her and call her your girlfriend, neither are you."

I walked back to where Julian, Chad, Eric and Jared and sat on Chad's lap.

"Awkward," Julian said and I laughed.

I turned to Eric and showed what I saw. His eyes widened and he nodded his head.

"What's going on," Chad asked.

I turned and whispered in his ear. "She's a part of the Blackness. Don't believe me ask Eric."

"I had a feeling she was," he said knowingly. "Does Dean know?"

I shook my head sadly and went to sit on Julian's lap. "We have to save Dean," I said to all of them. "If we don't, he won't be on our side anymore."

"That could be a problem," Jared said.

Chapter 11

I'm sitting in my room when a weird whooshing sound outside my window disturbs me. I thought Eric was trying to bother me because I was rehearsing but I don't think that's the case.

I started to get that familiar feeling at the pit of my stomach and I thought twice about going to the window. Appearing from thin air, a silver eyed demon flew into my window. At first he was just a mist until he fully materialized.

A tall boy with long blonde hair stood before me. He was about Julian's height and just as muscular. He eyes were really silver and they were corrupter by Blackness. He was a hottie but let's be honest: there are no ugly demons.

"Which one are you," I said sitting back on my bed and turning back to my script.

"The name's Brice," he said. His voice was nice and I sort of wished he wasn't evil. "You must be the famous Roel."

"That I am," I said giving him a sarcastic thumb up. "Are you here to kill me to because I'm really tired of threatening people and using my powers?"

He looked taken aback by my comment and thought for a moment. "Well I was here to try to hurt you but something doesn't seem right about that."

I looked at him furrowing my eyebrows. "What do you mean?"

"I thought you would put up a better fight," he said slowing sitting on my bed. "Is this some type of trap?"

I laughed and looked at him. "I'm too lazy to come up with a plan. Plus I'm rehearsing for this stupid play. If you don't mind, I can kind of sense when a demon is close and it makes me sick to my stomach," I gestured my hands to tell him to back off or go away.

I looked into his eyes and saw the Blackness losing its hold on him. "Can I ask you a question," he asked.

"You just did," I said jokingly and looked back into my book. "What?"

"Why does the Blackness want you dead," he asked stopping my breath and thought.

I looked at him and saw a glint of hope that would help him get away from that extra evil side. "I thought you demons wanted me dead. The Blackness is just quickening the process."

"Well I don't want you dead," he said closing his eyes. "I don't even like the darkness. It corrupted my brothers and it's corrupting me. Plus I think you're too pretty to die."

I looked at him skeptically and said, "That is sweet of you but if you're trying to butter me up you need to lose the Blackness first." I started to feel that uneasiness go away and it was a little relieving.

"I don't want the Blackness," he said and after that I couldn't believe what happened.

He started to scream and vein like strands of Blackness poured from his eyes. He fell to the ground in agonizing pain and the Blackness seeped out the window.

"Roel, what the," Julian's eyes went wide when he saw the demon who was now on his side in obvious pain. "What the hell happened?"

I didn't take my eyes off the demon that was on my floor. I shook my head to Julian because I really didn't know what happened. I slowly walked over to Brice but Julian stopped me.

"Ro stop," he said in a harsh whisper.

I shot a glaring glance at him and he let me go. I continued over to Brice before Julian could stop me this time. When I touched him his body went rigid like no one ever touched him before. When he relaxed he looked up at me with new eyes.

His eyes were a regular light grey and silver and they were quite breathtaking. His face looked completely different. His features were soft and inviting. He didn't look like a demon at that moment and I found him kind of adorable like Eric.

"Brice, are you okay," I asked and he looked at me confused.

"What, how did I get here," he asked looking around the room. "Who are you," he asked looking back at me.

I furrowed my eyebrows at him and Julian sat by my side. "My name is Roel. You came here to kill me."

"That's not cool," he said in a quiet voice. "I know you," he said looking at Julian. "You go to school with Blake. You're the dragon demons right?"

"Yea, dude," Julian laughed. Obviously he knew him. "What happened?"

I helped Brice to the bed and sat him down. "I was in my room listening to music when my brother, you know Blair, came into my room and threw something at me," he furrowed his eyebrows and looked into the window. "The next thing I remember is pain and darkness. Everything was black and weird."

"Well, you were here to kill me," I started, "but I didn't give you a care in the world and that confused the Blackness and then you came back to you."

"I remember some of that," he said looking at me. "I remember looking at you through the Blackness' eyes and seeing this pretty angel and I thought 'who in their right mind would want someone or something so beautiful dead?" he looked deep into my eyes and I felt a jolt of electricity flow through my body.

I blushed and smiled. "Thank you for that," I said holding his hands in mine. "Where's Blake?"

"He told me he was staying with a friend of his," he said. "He said his name was Chad."

I looked at Julian and he smiled. "I'll go get him," he said giving me a kiss on my forehead.

When Julian was out the door I sat down next to Brice. "How are you feeling?"

"Much better now," he said looking out the window. "I really didn't want to kill you." His hair cascaded down the side of his face. I pushed it aside and smiled at him.

"You know you can stay here if you want," I blurted out. "I mean there are some more empty rooms in the hell hole," I laughed bumping his shoulder with mine.

"If that's okay with your roommates," he said bumping my shoulder back.

"As long as you leave the Blackness behind you," Chad said from the door. He was giving Blake a seductive look and I knew that couldn't be right at all. "I'm Chad."

"Brice," he said. He looked at his brother and laughed. "So, I was right about you bro."

I looked between Chad, Blake and Brice and then Julian who had the same puzzled look on his face that I had.

139

"You were right," Blake said coldly. "What are you doing here," he asked in a controlled tone his hands becoming engulfed in flames.

"Chill out bro," Brice said blowing out the fire with air. "I'm not in alliance with that black shit. I was victimized."

Blake looked at his brother for a long time without making eye contact. "Damn I wish you were lying," he said putting his head on Chad's shoulder. I finally got it.

"You're gay too," I blurted before I could stop myself. "I didn't mean to blurt that out. It just finally clicked in my head. Blonde moment," I said hitting my forehead.

"Hey," Brice said dramatizing a broken heart. "I'm offended."

I laughed and covered my face. "Sorry about that," I said in a small voice.

"Can that Blackness come back" Julian asked.

"It can only corrupt immortals so humans will have no problems," Blake said moving away from Chad and checking on his brother. He looked into his eyes and felt on his cheeks. "You have faint scars where the Blackness came out. It burned you."

"How do you know so much about this Blackness," I asked skeptically.

"I saw it kill our mother," he said. "It almost took all the joy out of me but if it did that then it would've destroyed me. Chad saved me in a way with all of his happiness."

"How sweet," Julian said giving him a disgusted look. He walked over to me and pulled me into his arms. "How are you," he asked.

"I'm fine," I said looking up at him. His eyes looked sad and it pained me. "What's wrong?" When he didn't answer me I asked for everyone to clear the room.

When we were finally alone I sat him on my bed and stood in front of him. "Julian," I asked.

"I want a kiss," he said.

I kissed him on the cheek and he became flustered. "Is that it," I asked and laughed.

He smiled a little but it didn't reach his eyes. "Not that kind of kiss," he said seriously. "I want a real kiss."

"Julian," I groaned but he stopped.

"I'm becoming closed off again," he said a little angry. "I hate that feeling of being closed off from you. When I kiss you I can really tell you how I feel. I can really express myself to you." He looked at me with intense eyes but I couldn't look away. "The way your lips feel against mine makes me feel whole. It makes me feel like nothing in this world could go wrong."

I let those words sink in for a moment and tried to decide. "Fine," I said like a little girl. "I'll give you just one kiss."

He slowly worked his way to from my neck to my lips. When he kissed my lips my breath caught up in my chest and I forgot to move. I slowly kissed him back before moving my lips to the rhythm of his. At first the kiss was gentle and slow. He quickened the pace a little but kept in gentle.

I missed kissing him. I missed the feeling of complete peace and solace. He made me feel like there was no one else in the world but us. I wished it could've lasted longer but it had to be cut short.

I pulled away leaving both of us breathless. "Do you know how hard it is to refrain myself from ripping your close off right now," he asked me breathlessly.

"I can imagine," I said pointing to the risen bulge in his pants. "It must be really hard."

"That's not what I meant but that is a very good observation," he laughed taking my face in his hands and kissing me again. This time he stood.

This kiss was much hungrier and rougher. It intensified when he placed me on the bed under him and my legs wrapped around his hips. He wanted all of me but I didn't know if I was ready to give him everything.

"I'm scared," I whispered when he kissed my neck.

He stopped and looked into my eyes. His eyes were soft flames yet they were as intense as a fireplace fire. "I won't push you if you're not ready," he said sincerely.

"I want to," I said pushing him softly so I can get up. "I'm just scared of, you know," I said shyly.

"I get it," he said stroking my hair. "We don't have to. I don't want to rush you."

"You want to though," I argued. "You've done this plenty of times."

He laughed and shook his head. "That's where you're wrong, princess. I wasn't in love with the other girls so this would be completely different." He looked at his hand before he started talking. "With you, I'm afraid to hurt you. I'm afraid that if you're not ready then we'll have major issues. Also I want this to be perfect for you." He looked at me with so much love. "I'm irrevocably in love with you so making love to you would be new to me."

I looked at him with wide eyes. My eyes threatened with tears, I pulled him into a hug and held close. "I'm in love with you too," I whispered into his ear.

"Then I'll wait," he whispered back. "I want this to work and I want this to be perfect."

"Isn't that a shocker," an annoying familiar voice said from the door.

Instantly I burst into flame and my wings flew out. "What the hell are you doing here," I said in my scary voice.

"I came with Liz," Julia said with a smile on your face. "Look at you being all scary."

I calmed myself and put my wings back. "Get the hell out of my room, my house, get the hell out!"

"I'm sorry but I'm not your company," she said with a sneer.

I looked into her eyes and found the Blackness and something more. Her eyes were red. I tried to suck the air out of her lungs but she didn't seem to mind. *She's a vampire,* I thought to myself. I smirked and engulfed her in flames. She started screaming like a crazy banshee and fell to the floor.

She was in the hallway screaming in pain when everyone found her. I was standing over her laughing evilly making the scene more cynical.

"Julia," Elizabeth screamed running over to her burning friend. "Stop, you're hurting her," she yelled at me.

I stopped torturing Julia and turned my attention to Elizabeth. "Why should I have stopped?"

The Blackness in her eyes intensified and she flew toward me. She started to choke me and I realized something. "Only immortals can be corrupted by the Blackness."

Her body disappeared and left nothing but a shadow of Blackness. "I am the Blackness," she said in this unknown voice.

"Great," I said before I passed out.

to come to you full, full powers but invoking spirit and shutting Canicus out for now."

"How do I do that?"

"With spirit, comes life," she said and I started to feel myself going back into my body. "When you go back to your body you'll figure out how to save yourself and them."

I was back in my body and my senses snapped me conscious. I looked at the shadow figure and realized what my mom meant. This figure was a Death of sorts. I was temporarily trapped within a world between life and death and I could feel I was close to being dead. All I had to is turn that against her.

I stood and felt myself fade into a white version of her shadow. "Hey," I said causing wide eyes to fall on me. "Stay away from my boys," I said and a flash of light burned through Canicus with a piercing sound.

The flash was bright enough to blind me for about a brief moment. When the light dimmed I realized that Canicus was gone and was replaced with Elizabeth again. She fell to the ground with a thump and started to shake.

I felt a little too free for a moment and realized that I was still in my mist and Spirit form.

Everyone was checking on each other and Elizabeth to be worried about the white mist standing by the wall. Everyone but Julian that is.

"Roel," he whispered causing me to snap back into my body.

"Huh," I said a little bewildered. I shook my head knowing what his question would be. I didn't know what happened to me.

I looked down to see that Dean was coxing Elizabeth and rubbing her head. Julia was still unconscious on the floor and I wondered if she was still being possessed by the Blackness.

"Stand back," I said as Julia stirred on the ground.

Everyone complied as she jumped up from the ground and landed in a crouch.

"What the hell did you do to me," she hissed behind her teeth. Wait . . . Are those fangs? I forgot she was a vampire already.

"I didn't do anything," my voice held something that was completely new and I was compelled by the sound. I looked in her eyes and realized that the darkness was still harboring in her body.

"You need to leave," Julian said coming next to me. "You were never invited."

She smiled slyly and I realized that she'd become Canicus. "You don't have to invite the darkness. When the child is already dark in essence then they will comply with anything." She turned toward and smiled showing her fangs. "You, my child, are very wise. You knew only in your Spirit form can you put me back in a body. Thankfully none of your precious boys were unconscious because things would've gotten really nasty." She turned to Dean and gave him a knowing smile. "I still have a good hold on her," he said putting her hand on Elizabeth's head. "She'll never be back to normal."

"You son of a bitch," I said using the power of spirit to tear Canicus from Julia's body. "You have the nerve to think you can hurt us with the state you're in."

Canicus laughed and took on a body of its own. It was an older looking guy, probably about twenty five. His hair was almost as long as mine and just as black. He was taller than Dean. I felt he towered over me. His skin was a mix of brown and orange. He was the epitome of what gorgeous should look like. I guessed that's what made him so alluring.

"Little girl," he chuckled as he gracefully glided toward. "I've been around before your ancestors were thought about. I have many states that I can make myself into." The hold I had on him diminished and he took me by the throat. "You, my darling, are far below my standards of what I should be fighting against."

"Then actually fight me then," I said losing breath that I was trying to hold on to. "Fight me instead of trying and failing to kill me. It seems that you won't be able to manage that."

He put me down lightly and smiled again. "You are far too weak for a fair fight," he said meekly. "I'll give you a month's time to actually be able to figure out how to use your power. Then when the time is right we will see if you have what it takes to kill me." He disappeared taking Julia and Elizabeth with him.

He was right about one thing. I was beyond weak right now. I fell on my knees and felt the exhaustion overwhelm me. Julian was back by my side at an instant along with the rest of my boys including Blake and Brice.

"I'm sleepy," I said closing my eyes. "Sleep sounds really good right now."

Julian laughed absently. "Get some rest Ro," he said kissing my forehead. "We'll work tomorrow."

Chapter 13

"Ow," I yelled as Julian tried to burn me to a crisp. "That hurts if you didn't notice."

"Sorry," he said picking me off the basement floor. "You need to learn how to turn an attack on your opponent."

"Well it's not working," I said shaking him off. "Again," I yelled getting back into the stance he taught me.

"You need to rest a bit," he ordered pushing me into a chair. "You've been pushing yourself for the last week."

"Where is the punching bag," I said getting up from the chair. "I need to punch something."

"No," he said and I punched him in the mouth. "What the hell was that for," he yelled holding his jaw.

I shook my hand because it felt like I just hit a fucking brick wall. "I told you I needed to punch something," I informed him. "Now get the fucking punching bag."

He straightened up and threw a ball of flames at me. I caught it and threw it back at him causing him to fly into the wall.

"What are you lovebirds doing," Dean said coming down the stairs with food. "Well it looks like Julian's getting his ask kicked," he yelled up the stairs.

"Julian won't give me the punching bag," I said crossing my arms and glaring at Julian.

He got up from the floor and smiled. "You accomplished something though," he said walking over to me. "You used my attack against me."

Still glaring at him I smiled a little. "You should've gotten me the damn punching bag."

"Well you can punch all you want now," he said wrapping his arms around me. "My jaw will heal."

I rested my head on his chest and sighed. "A trip to my room would be nice," I said grabbing his butt in the process.

He jumped and backed out of my arms. "Hands off if I can't touch," he said shaking his finger.

"You can touch all you want," I said seductively. "But seriously, I want to go to my room and lay down."

"Ladies first," he said bowing to the stairs.

I gave him a curtsy and walked up the stair looking like a warrior version of a Victorian princess. "Thanks good sir, Julian," I said with a British accent.

"Anything for my lady, Roel," he said matching my accent.

We really sounded like some shit out of a Shakespeare play and it weirded me out. When I got upstairs it looked like world war three just went through the house.

"What the hell happened," I said slowly and a little angry.

"Eric and Brice got into it," Dean said from behind me. "They are in the living room now."

I went into the living and found Brice and Eric standing across from each other getting ready to fight again. I sent both of them into the opposite walls and then they hit the floor.

"Are you two insane or just plain stupid," I said. "The answer better be good."

"Eric started it," Brice yelled getting up from the floor.

"Did not," Eric yelled.

"Did too."

"Did not."

"Shut up."

"Go to hell."

"I'll follow you."

"Shut the hell up, both of you," I yelled taking the air from both of them. "Goodness, you two sound like two big ass babies crying over who stole the last fucking cookie. Grow the hell up!"

"Tell Blake to grow up," Eric said dusting off his shirt.

"Bite me," Brice said.

"How about I beat the shit out of you?"

I threw both of them into the wall again and they groaned from the pain. "If you two don't shut up I'm going to beat the shit out of both of you," I said as my eyes flamed up. "Eric, go to your room and calm down. Brice, go take a walk." When they both didn't move I barked, "Now."

They glared at each other for another moment and parted ways. I watched as Eric went to his room and Brice walked out the front door.

I looked at the rest of the boys who were staring at me with fear in their eyes. "Julian and I are going upstairs. If I wake up and this house is not clean, I'm going to burn the shit out of all of you."

They started moving once my sentence was finished. As I went upstairs Eric came down and helped clean up.

When I got to my room I shot up in flames from all the held up anger. Julian let me fume before he turned me around and planted a kiss on my lips. I melted in his embrace and the flames subsided.

"You know, you have a really bad temper," he said when he pulled him lips away from mine.

"I get it from my hot headed boyfriend," I said kissing him again. This time I kissed him slow and tempting causing a problem to rise in his pants. If I had one, I'd so be sporting major wood right now.

"Do you always have to do that," he said trying to control the shaking in his voice. "I don't like it when you tease me."

"Do something about it," I said and pushed him into the door. "Make me stop teasing you." I kissed his neck causing a moan to escape from his chest.

"Stop it," he said pushing me away from him weakly. When I didn't stop he pushed me in the bed and got on top of me.

"Ohh, someone's getting hot and feisty," I said pulling off his shirt and flipping him over.

"I'm the one that's feisty," he asked as I bit his neck. "You're the one biting and teasing."

I laughed as he flipped me back over. "I know but you're the one with the wood." I pointed to the bulge in his pants.

When I reached for his pants he stopped me. "Wait," he said getting off of me and sitting on the bed. "You're really ready to do this. I know we've talked about this for a week but are you really ready to give yourself to me?"

I looked into his eyes and smiled weakly. "I think I am. I just want to have you in every way."

He smiled softly and took my hand in his. "You can have me in every way shape and form. But when you know that you're completely ready for it." He kissed my hand and pulled me back into him. "I think we can do other things that would get us ready for that time."

For hours we sat in the shower just holding each other. There was nothing that could take me away from this moment. How perfect we fit together while standing there. How warm his body was on mine. It was like being free from all the pain, doubt, and hurt of the world. It was just me and him, a boy and a girl.

"I love you," I said into his chest.

"I love you too," he said into my hair. "You made me feel, I don't even know how to explain. I've never experienced anything like that in my life."

"You're lying," I said looking up at him.

"I'm serious. I've never just been with a girl before and it was amazing that it was with you." He kissed me and I smiled under his lips. "Your body is amazing."

"Your body is equally amazing."

"Thanks," he laughed kissing my forehead. "Do you want to sleep?"

I was already nodding off before we started talking but I nodded anyway. "Make sure they cleaned up because I'm in too good of a mood to burn my brothers."

"Anything for you, my lady," he said and got up.

"Nice butt," I said. "Don't go out my room like that. Only I get to see that."

"I'll remember that," he said.

I smiled at him before he kissed my forehead and went to the bathroom. I fell asleep before I knew it.

Chapter 14

"Roel stop now," Julian said as I punched the punching bag. "You're gonna break your wrists or something."

I ignored him and kept punching. I was reeling due to the fact that I was soon facing the stupid Blackness, Canicus, and I wasn't ready. Also my mom has been getting into my dreams and it was annoying.

"You try having someone talking you to death in your sleep while you're being threatened by Canicus," I said enunciating every word while I punched. "On top of all of that I have to be in a play and I hate acting. Step in my shoes for a moment, will ya?"

"You're making everyone around you suffer," he said getting in the way of the bag. "Eric's had a headache for the last two weeks. Give it a break." He caught my hand before it could connect with his face. "I said stop."

I wriggled under his touch because it was colder than it should have been. "Let me go," I said through clenched teeth.

"Not until you promise to stop for the day," he said through his teeth.

"He's right," Chad said coming down the stairs. "You're really giving Eric a headache with all your bitterness. Where did it all come from?"

"Mind your business," I said to him. "I promise I won't train anymore today."

"Promise," he asked again.

"I said I promise."

He let my hand go and I back away from him. I started toward the stairs but he stopped me.

"Where are you going," he asked softly.

"To my room," I said trying to control my anger. "I promise I won't do anything stupid. I'm just going to rest."

"You want me to-"

"No," I said too quickly. "No, I need to talk to Eric and apologize."

He looked a little sad so I pulled myself to him and gave him a reassuring kiss. "I hope you'll be okay," he said kissing my forehead.

"I just need to understand why my mom is driving me nuts right now," I said and kissed him again.

I went into the living room to find Eric, Dean and Jared sitting around watching TV. Eric had his head against his knees. I could tell he was in some serious pain.

"Eric," I said softly. "Can I talk to you?"

He looked up at me with blood shot red eyes. "Sure," he said in a pained voice.

I tried to keep my thoughts calm and relaxed while I walked to my room but it didn't manage to work.

"The ocean isn't helping much," he said to me when I closed my door. "It's making me nauseas."

"I'm sorry," I said. We haven't really talked since he was hurt badly by Blair and his brothers. "How are you? Don't answer that."

"No, I'm fine," he said sitting down on the bed. "I need sleep but I can't get sleep when you're having bad dreams and even worse thoughts."

"I know. That's what I wanted to talk to you about." I sat next to him on the bed and looked down at my twitching fingers. "You know how my mom said the only way to drive away Canicus is through Spirit and Light? How do I do that?"

"You have to listen to her," he said rubbing his temples. "You know only you and her knows that answer and for the simple fact that she's not telling you means that you have to find out on your own."

I sighed heavily. "I knew you'd say that."

"You can read minds too," he joked.

"No but my mom said the same thing but it was more annoying coming from her," I said. "Why did she come to help me if she won't explain to help me?"

"I don't know Roel," he said putting his hand on my shoulder. "You'll find a way though. I know you will."

"I wish I had that much confidence in myself." Truth is I didn't have any confidence that I could do this. "I still can't do this without you guys."

"You'll never have to do anything without me," he said kissing my forehead. "You're my best friend. I can't ever betray you."

"Thanks Eric," I said hugging him. "And I'm really sorry for putting all of this stress on you."

"No problem," he said. "Talking to you made me feel a lot better."

"Happy to help," I said. "I'll try not to think or worry too much."

"It's all good," he said getting up and heading for the door. "I'll let you get some rest. We'll figure this out together. You're never alone."

He closed the door and I sprawled myself out on the bed. "I hope I'm not in this alone." I closed my eyes to see a very familiar face.

"What the hell do you want," I yelled at her.

"That's how you talk to your mom," she asked sitting her chair. When I fall asleep she brings me to this house that looks like something out of the medieval times. She has the big chair that sits in front of a fire place and an end table. She always has a cup of tea and some fancy shit going on but it just annoys the hell out of me.

"You brought me here, you want something," I said crossing my arms and sitting in the chair across from her. My chair wasn't as fancy as hers but it was cool for me.

"Why is it so hard to believe that I just want to spend time with you," she asked with a hint of sadness in her eyes.

I barked a laugh and gave her a humored look. "After fourteen years of not being there now you want to spend time with me? Why don't you hop in Chad's dreams? He would love to know to see you."

"I can't get into his dreams, Roel," she said getting a little angry. "I'm in yours because I need your help."

"Why do you need my help?"

"Because if you don't get to me after you defeat Canicus then I'll die."

Chapter 16

"You've been bugging me for a week and now you tell me that you're gonna die," I yelled at her. "What the hell took you so long to tell me?"

"I didn't want to burden you," she informed me like it was a simple matter. "You had a lot on your plate."

"News flash mom; NONE OF THAT HAS CHANGED," I threw up my hands in frustration. "You are so impossible."

"I had to tell you before you went to face Canicus," she sounded tired and I realized that her face was a little paler than usual.

"Mom, are you okay," I asked and crouched down in front of her.

She smiled weakly at me trying to put on a safe face. "I'm dying, Roel. My body is still in the real world but I can't get back to it. I've been fading from this world too."

I took some time to let her words sink in. "Where's your body," I asked in a quiet voice.

"Do you think I'd be here if I knew?"

"Well, no, but how do you expect me to find it? I'm not that good at finding things."

"A piece of my spirit is still connected to my body," she said rubbing my head. I may be mad at her but she's still my mom. "I was able to control the element to spirit and I can teach you how to use is."

"I'm listening," I said and put my head in her lap.

"Okay well right after you wake up I want you to meditate."

"How is that-"

"Let me finish," she cut me off. "When you're meditating I want you to call on spirit and ask it to restore my body to my soul after Canicus is killed. Then I'll be able to restore myself and find you guys again." She waved her hand over the fire and a portal showed my boys in the living room watching TV. "They love you very much Ro," she said looking at them with a distant stare. "You should cherish them and make them see you love them in return."

"I do make them see, mom," I said in a quiet tone. "I just feel so alone. I feel like it's me against the world sometimes."

"Darling I'm always here with you," she said in that motherly voice. "You're never alone anyway. You have five, actually seven if you count Brice and Blake, boys who truly love you for who you are and what you do."

"But they aren't the ones I want to love me like that," I said looking up at her all child-like.

"Sweetie not a day goes by when I don't think about you or stopped loving you," she said taking my face in her hands. "You and Chad are the only reasons I'm still alive and don't you ever forget that."

A silent tear fell from my eye at the same time as hers. "Mom I'm sorry," I said getting up to give her a hug.

"It's okay," she said embracing me. "You'll help me. You'll be able to fix this."

"Why does everyone have that much confidence in me," I asked putting my head back on her knee. "What if I mess up?"

She laughed lightly. "Trust me, Roel, you will not mess up. I have confidence in you because I know you can do it. I believe in you."

"After all these years you believe in me now," I said sarcastically.

"Do you always have to be so damn sarcastic?"

"It's my first language," I joked.

"Oh, darling," she smiled. "You are a bright child. You will bring the balance of good and bad back around. I know you will."

I felt myself drifting back into the real world. "I love you mom," I said before the dream completely disappeared. I felt groggy and sore when I woke up. I opened my eyes to a bright sun from the window. I closed my eyes and tried to put myself back to sleep. It didn't work and someone knocked on my door.

"What do I have to get some much needed sleep around here," I yelled going to the door. I swung open the door and Julian stood with a really surprised looking face on.

"Did someone wake on the wrong side of the bed," he asked. "You slept through most of the day and I wanted to check and see if you killed yourself or something."

"I'm not dead yet," I said walking back to my bed. "I'm just really tired and sore."

He came and sat beside me. "Well the soreness is your fault." I shot him an evil stare and he put his hands up. "You're the one who wanted to work out and train and beat the life out of a punching bag."

"I have to be ready for Canicus," I said putting my head on his shoulder. "I'm not sure that I'm going to be able to beat him."

He stroked my hair and kissed my head. "You are going to beat him. Ayez la foi mon amour."

"What the hell did you just say," I asked him jokingly.

"Have faith, my love," he said laughing. "You should have faith in yourself."

"Where did you learn French?"

"I'm in a play called Romeo and Juliet. You didn't believe I wouldn't learn at least one language from England." He looked at me and smiled. "Plus French is one of the most romantic languages a person can know."

"I'm sure," I laughed. "And you are the epitome of romance."

"I can only try, right," he said.

"Why do you have so much faith in me?"

His face became serious and his eyes intense. "You're my girl, that's why. You changed this house with your personality and whit. You changed me as a person. You chased the Blackness out of Brice by making him feel love and your personality. And trust me that boys loves you." He laughed a little and I joined him. "You have the power to make everything bright when everything is dark. You're the opposite of Canicus is and what he does. That's why I have so much faith in you."

"You know you can be a serious romantic," I laughed and kissed him on the lips. "I'm happy that you're happy. You make me feel so good."

"I try," he said putting on a cocky grin. "I love you Roel. I hope you never forget that."

I looked at him with the serious face. "How can I forget that? I love you too Julian." I gave him a cocky grin and said, "Je vous aime."

"Oh, so you think you know French," he laughed. "And you were talking about me."

"I can only try." As long as my family has faith in me nothing can go wrong.

161

Then again I have the moments where I'm wrong. This time I could've been. Something crashed through my window and shattered glass toward me and Julian.

"What the hell," Julian yelled at the black figure on the floor in the middle of my room.

The figure materialized itself into Canicus. "Hello, Roel and the orange beast."

"What the hell do you want," I said instantly flaming up and spreading my wings. "You're not welcome here."

"You are being so rude to your guest," he said with mock disappointment. "I'm here because I wanted to make a deal. A proposition of sorts," he sat on my bed like there was nothing wrong with an all-powerful demon flying through a window.

"You broke my window to make a deal with me," I said a little amused. "Why didn't you just use the front door?"

He laughed like I was supposed to know that already. "You should know that I like to make a scene."

I watched him intently and saw Julian in the corner of my eye. He was shaking with visible anger. You could tell he wanted to burn the hell out of Canicus.

I put my hand on his chest to calm him down and he instantly became at ease but still alert. "What kind of proposition," I asked looking at Canicus again.

"A life for a life," he said simply. "Your mom is dying am I right?"

The flames that engulfed me turned bright orange and my hair turned red. "What did you do to her," I asked.

"She's fine. She's not dead yet."

"I know that, you dirt bag," I said with a controlled voice. "You will tell me what you did to her."

"She made a deal," he said giving me an evil grin. "She wants to spear your life for hers."

"I'm not letting that happen," I said and threw a ball of energy and flames at him. He quickly dodged it but I slammed him against the wall and got in his face. "You have opened a whole new can of worm, you mongrel. If you came here to see if I make the same deal then let me cut this visit short. I'm not as stupid as my mother is. I don't make deals with the devil. You may not be as badass as you think but you have no power over me.

"You will leave here and we will make plans for the war that you have created. The battles that I've been through left me with three points and you know. If you think you have power over me or my mom then you must be as stupid as the last demon who tried to kill me. He could've been burned to a crisp. You're gonna lose. And I hope you remember that."

He laughed and threw me across the room. "I hope your losing speech is way better than that. You cannot beat me and you never will be able to. I hope you remember that." He shot something at me and it blurred my eyes. He was out the window in that same instant.

"JULIAN I CAN'T SEE," I yelled thrashing my hands frantically. I tried to open my eyes but I felt a hand go over them.

"Don't open your eyes," he yelled as he slowly picked me up off the floor. "Roel, you have to calm down." I kept flailing my hands trying to get the inkiness off my eyes. "It's Blackness Roel," he said and I abruptly stopped. "You can't open your eyes because there is Blackness over them. If you open them you will consume it. I sure as hell know you don't want to do that."

I silently started crying. "Get me to them," I said slowly. "I need all of your help to get this off."

"Ok," he said. "Follow me."

"Did any of it get on you," I asked taking his hand.

He paused and I knew he was checking his body. "No it's all on your face and it's spreading. Close your mouth. It can only affect you if it gets in your mouth and eyes." He took my hand and started quickly out of my room. "Help us," he yelled. I felt everyone stumble into the hallway moments after. "Canicus came and threw the Blackness on her face."

Chad was the first one to me as always. "We need to get her in the sun," he said picking me of and dashing down the stairs. "It will hopefully disintegrate in the sunlight."

"And what if it doesn't," Julian asked right behind Chad. I heard the footsteps of the rest of them behind him.

"Then she will have to fight Canicus blind."

Chapter 17

Stuck wasn't even the word to explain how I felt. It was more like I was cement glued to Chad's arms. He was moving me so fast that I felt numb.

"I'm going to be blind," I asked absently.

"No you will not," Chad demanded. I felt the sun hit my skin but it didn't cut through the thick Blackness that was consuming my face.

"Is it bad," I asked after a while. The inky black stuff didn't subside and it didn't lighten up.

"It's not all over your face anymore," Chad said caressing the side of my face.

"Maybe I can wash it off," I heard Jared say.

I felt the soothing water run on my face. It was calming and reassuring. The Blackness lightened up a little but I still couldn't see.

"It will take days, maybe weeks before you can get this stuff fully off," Jared said still trying to help my eyes. "I'll work on it every day for an hour."

"This so totally sucks major blue balls," I said jumping out of Chad's arms. "I fucking hate my life."

"Don't worry, love," Jared said taking my hand and releasing his element from my face. "We will get the bastard for this shit."

"If he wins I'm going to burn this entire city to hell." I meant that figuratively but I can tell they thought I was serious. "I didn't mean literally."

"We know that," Eric said. He shook himself mentally. "You have to use your other senses for a while. You might be able to go to school tomorrow."

"I'm going to school blind. Great," I threw up my hand s and walked into what seemed like a brick wall.

Two warm, giant hands caught my shoulder before I fell back. "You know it's kind of hard to walk through a person."

"Thanks for the update Brice," I said holding onto his forearms. He was not as warm as Julian but he always left my heart warm after he touched me.

"Are we just gonna stand here while she's fighting with this Blackness or are we going to teach her to use her other senses?" Chad grabbed my hand and whirled me in the house. I could feel that he was going to the basement and I had a feeling of what we were doing.

"Eric, stand at the west point of the basement." Chad was still holding my hand and I could feel his spirit buzzing around me. "Dean, stand at the north point. Julian, you take the east point and Jared the south. I'll stay in the middle with Ro."

"What's going on," I asked looking in the direction of his voice.

"You may have to fight Canicus blind so in that case you need to know where the attack is coming from." Chad held both of my hands. "Right now we're going to see if you can find out where an attack is going to come from."

"I guess," I said and turned away from him.

"Julian, attack her," Chad said. It was silent for a long moment. "We don't have time for hesitation. I said attack."

Without any more hesitation I felt Julian launch himself at me. I slid to the side just in time to feel the heat of Julian's body.

He hit the wall with so much force that it shook the house. "What the hell are doing, trying to kill me," I yelled.

"I was just doing what Chad said," Julian said. "It's not like I was going to hurt you."

"Like hell you weren't," I yelled back at him. "You put a whole in the wall."

"You can't even see so how would you know," Brice said from what I thought were the stairs.

"I heard the wall break, smart ass," I said to him. "I may not be able to see but I can hear, smell, taste and feel everything around me. You think I can't hear a wall break? Give me a freaking break."

"Well, excuse me miss know it all," he said in a slick tone.

"Bite me," I said crossing my arms. "I'm blind not deaf."

"What can you taste," Chad said ignoring the arguing.

"The heat radiating off of everyone's body," I started. "I can taste the dirt in the air and it's nasty."

"Well besides that," he interrupted.

"I don't know okay," I yelled in frustration. "I'm tired and my eyes hurt because they're closed so tight." I sat on the floor and crossed my arms and legs. "I want to be alone," I said quietly. "Maybe I can tune into the elements better if I concentrate and meditate."

"Let's leave her be," Chad said quietly. "We'll check on you later."

"Fine," I said.

When they all left the basement I wept silently. "I'm freaking blind for crying out loud," I whispered. "I ask anyone who can hear me. I need help with this asshole. I don't want to lose against some cheating cunt bag who won't fight fair."

Lanaya A. Pickett

I tilted my head back as if I was looking toward the sky. "If there is any way to beat him while I'm blind, please help me find that way."

I sat there and waited for the answer.

Chapter 18

There's nothing like a day of silence when you can't see anything. The only problem is that nothing is silent. Everything is so loud. I can hear birds chirping from outside my window. My window is closed and there are no birds in that tree. I can hear Julian in his room playing video games. Chad's in his room watching pretty woman with Blake. Their cuddling and doing other things that I find utterly disturbing. Dean's filling out some type of paper work and the pen going across the paper is driving me crazy.

I heard footsteps outside my door but I answered before they could knock. "Come in," I yelled.

Eric walked in calmly but I could tell he was on edge. "How are you," he asked in an all too silent tone.

"I'm fine," I lied. "I'm blind and my ears feel like they're about to bleed."

"I understand," he said. "Jared wants to know if he can do the cleansing now."

"I don't care," I said looking toward the window. I wished I could see outside because I could feel the sun streaming through my window and I knew it was a beautiful sight.

I heard Jared walked in my room. His footsteps were light and adoring just like him. "Hey, Ro," he said sitting next to me.

"Dude, you smell like you were in a men's colon store for hours."

"Is it that strong," he asked. I heard him sniff himself and I laughed.

"I'm blind and my other senses are heightened a little," I said bumping his shoulder. "You smell good by the way."

"Thanks," he said. He slid his hand across my face and I felt the soft healing powers of water go to work.

"That feels good," I said softly.

The last few days have been very stressful. I couldn't be anywhere in school without an escort. I didn't want to eat anything because, well, because everything tasted like crap. I hated smelling everything and hearing everything. My ears have been hurting because of all the freaking sound waves flowing through them. The only time I could get away from all of that is when I'm with Jared. Not with Jared like that but when he's healing me. Everything becomes silent and normal. It feels really good.

"How long do you want to do it this time," he asked after a long quiet moment.

"A while," I sighed. "I want to just relax for a while."

"There is a better way to do this," he said quietly.

"Like hell there is," Julian said from the door. "You put your lips on her and I'm going to kick your goofy ass."

The healing sensation went away and a burst of heat flooded my face. "What the hell, Julian," I yelled.

"His little healing power works better if he kisses you," he said in a clipped tone. "That's really not going to happen."

"I was just trying to help," Jared argued. "It's not like I'm going to try to take her away from you."

"You have something for her and you know it," Julian yelled back.

They started arguing and yelling like I wasn't in the room. Everything was way too loud. It sounded like thousands of footsteps were running down the hall. Everyone flooded in my room to see the two fuming boys.

"HEY," Eric and I yelled. "I can freaking hear you!" I turned my face toward them. If I could see then I'd so be glaring at them. "Everyone needs to get downstairs now," I said in an angry tone. When I heard a lot of shuffling and movement I yelled, "Quietly."

Eric took my hand and led me downstairs. I was angry and he could feel it. He was trying to comfort me but it just wasn't working. I was beyond pissed.

"Sit down," I said as Eric sat me down on the couch. "Explain to me why the hell you two wanted to fight upstairs."

Both Julian and Jared started to talk at the same time so I filled their lungs with water. "Can you speak one at a time," I asked.

When I was sure they were going to act right I released the water from their lungs and let them explain. "He thinks that kissing you will heal you better," Julian said first. "He's just trying to make a move on you."

"Jared," I turned to Jared to hear his side of the situation.

"I'm not trying to make a pass at you," he said softly.

"Bullshit," Julian yelled and I cut him off.

"Shut up," I said in a clipped tone. "You said your piece now let Jared talk."

"But he's lying."

"I said shut it." I turned back to Jared. "How does kissing me help the healing process?"

"I'll be able to fill your body with the element and it will fight the Blackness from the inside," he sighed. "I can teach you how to do it yourself but that will take too long and you need to be in tuned with your sight when you go up against Canicus."

I contemplated his words for a moment. "Julian, come here," I said quietly. I felt his heat brush my face before his hand did. I stood up to hug him. "Let him help me. If he can fix this enough to where I can see a little then I might have a chance to kill or badly damage Canicus."

I felt his body stiffen and his nerves jump. He was radiating with anger and it annoyed me that he didn't trust me enough. "I don't know-"

"Julian," I said getting a little angry. "This isn't about me and you. It's about me actually surviving this battle. Yes, I love Jared," I said and Julian almost pulled away from me but I held him tight. "But, I'm in love with you. Jared's just a brother to me. He's like one of my best friends. You can't ever change that. But you have to know that you're the only one who has my heart."

He was quiet for a moment and then he said, "Fine but just this one time." He kissed my lips and I smiled. "You make me so angry sometimes."

"I'm you girlfriend," I said and kissed him again. "It's my duty to piss you off. Jared, come here," I turned to where Jared was standing and I felt the cooling sensation of water flow over to me. "If this works then I'll owe you. If this is just a way to kiss me I will make sure you burn a thousand times over."

"I promise that I'm not going to do anything stupid," he said. I pictured he was putting his hand over his heart and bowing to me or something. "We need to sit down," he pulled me over to the love couch. "They can stay in here if they think I'm gonna do something stupid."

"Damn right we're staying," Julian said coming to stand by my side.

I shook my head and smiled. "Throughout all of this mess, you still manage to act like boys. It amazes me that I'm still here."

"It's because we're all so freaking charming," Chad laughed.

"Focus, Roel," Jared said. "I'm going to push some of my energy of water through you to help your element."

"Okay," I said nervously.

"Don't be scared," he said taking my hand. "You're not the one being threatened to be burn a thousand times over."

I laughed and nodded my head. "Let's do this," I said.

I felt his cool lips inching toward mine and a rush of butterflies filled my body. When our lips met a cool liquid feeling flowed from his mouth to mine. Wherever it touched I left a tingling sensation. It was so sweet.

The best thing about it was the taste of his mouth. It tasted of the salty ocean but it wasn't a nasty taste. It felt like I was actually being filled with ocean water.

The tingling flowing through my body finally reached my eyes. At first I wanted to pull away from Jared because it started to hurt my eyes but soon after the pain was replaced by a calming bliss. Both of our elements were at work and I felt it slowly working on my eyes. I felt relaxed and rejuvenated.

When he finally pulled away he left a small space between us but he was still close enough to where I could feel his lips turn up into a smile. "You can open your eyes now," he whispered.

I slowly opened my eyes and saw the outline of Jared's face. I couldn't see much but I could make out his breath taking blue eyes. "I can see your eyes. I can't see your entire face."

"It didn't work all the way," he said pulling away from me fully. "You can see eyes but you may not be able to see everything."

"But it worked," I said blinking my eyes. "I can see some things." I looked up at Julian and smiled. "I can see the heat flowing through your body," I said taking his hands. I closed my eyes again and then looked into his eyes. "Your eyes are so pretty," I said kissing him on the cheek. "You have no idea how repulsive it is to kiss him," I joked.

He was giving me a weird look and I was slightly confused. "Your eyes are kind of black," he said. "They look weird."

"Well thanks Ju-ju," I said turning away from you. "I can finally see and you're calling me weird."

"They're still beautiful," he defended. "They just look different."

I turned back toward him and smiled. I could see finally and I was glad that I could see him. He looked just the same but it brought me joy to actually see him. I smiled and tried to walk but I fell into his arms. "I'm sleepy."

I turned to Jared to find him fast asleep on the couch. "That's another side effect," Eric said taking me in his arms. "She'll be fine after some rest and sleep. You guys can check on her in the morning."

He put my arm over his shoulder and started walking up the stairs. "You have gray eyes," I said looking at him.

"They haven't changed, Ro."

"I thought they were silver," I said groggily. "Either way you're eyes are beautiful. Why is it I can see eyes better than I can see anything else?"

He laughed and we reached my room. He sat me on my bed and I fell back. "Eyes are the gateway to

174

someone's soul. You can see eyes because you can see the real them."

"Oh," I sighed. I turned on my side and smiled up at Eric. "You're my bestest friend, Eric. You're always there for me."

"All of us are always there for you," he smiled sitting down next to me. "I'm your closest friend."

"Yea, that's what you are," I said closing my eyes. I started slipping into a deep slumber. "I love you Eric," I said softly.

"Anything for my best friend," he said kissing my forehead.

Chapter 19

"Hi mom," I said coming into her dream living room.

"I see you're feeling better," she said weakly. "How are your eyes in the real world?"

"They're better," I said rubbing them. "They've gotten better since the healing kiss. You, however, look like crap."

She laughed lightly and said, "I feel like crap. Have you found out how to defeat Canicus?"

"Honestly, no I haven't," I said sitting down in my chair. "How can I kill without changing the balance of good and evil?"

"You can't kill him per 'say,'" she said. "You can only bring the balance back to normal. As long as your new friends keep becoming good, you will have to worry about the bad getting worse. You can kill Canicus but that would only create an even worse problem."

"You mean something is worse than Canicus?"

"Of course," she said and then coughed.

"Mom, why won't you tell me where you are," I said coming to her side. "You're getting really sick and I'm scared that I won't get to you in time."

"And that's why I won't tell you, she retorted. "Do you not get it? Family is your weakness and Canicus knows that now. Every time someone you know and love gets hurt you break down and get angry. Getting angry can be good at times but if you let him get to you then you'll end up losing."

"So you're not gonna tell me where you are because you think I'm going to come get you now," I asked her. "I'm more than capable of knowing that it wouldn't be smart to get you now."

"I know you know that." Her body looked frail as she stood up from the chair. "You have to at least get Canicus away from me before you go and try to save me."

I heard loud noise and screams coming from outside of my head. "Mom, I have to go," I said closing my eyes.

"You'll find me, she said before I woke up.

Something was crushing my lungs and I couldn't breathe at all. Julian, I realized, was shielding me from something and I couldn't figure out what.

"JULIAN YOU'RE CRUSHING ME," I yelled. He looked down at me in shock. "GET UP!"

He jumped off me and ran to shut the door. "Why weren't you waking up," he asked holding the door from whatever was on the other side.

"I was with my mom," said giving his eyes a weird look. "What's going on?"

"Canicus's here," he said and the door burst open.

There he was holding Eric by the throat. He looked every bit of angry and menacing.

I went to grab Julian from the floor. He was holding his side which was covered in blood. He had a large piece of glass sticking out of it.

I went to grab Eric from Canicus but he pulled him back. "If you touch him, he dies," he said in an extra creepy demon voice. "I'm tired of waiting for you."

I flamed up and my wings flew out from behind me. "Let him go," I said in a dark tone. "This is between you and me."

"Fine," he said and threw Eric toward me. "Find me at the island." He pushed me out the window with his mind and took Julian. Then with a blink of an eye, he vanished taking Julian with him.

Before I could hit the ground my wings extended and I flew back to my window. Eric was lying on the floor unconscious and my room was a disaster. I was assuming that the rest of the house was the same.

"Eric," I yelled flying over to him. I took his face in my hands and smacked him a few times. "Eric, please wake up," I yelled louder. He woke groggily and I was happier than ever to see his eyes.

"Roel, are you okay," he asked in a battered voice. He sounded broken and badly hurt.

"I'm fine," I said picking him up off the floor. "Where is everyone else?"

"They went to the island already," he said after almost coughing up a lung. "The demons lured them. We have to go now."

I looked to the ground where Julian fell and found a pool of blood. "Oh gosh," I said feeling dizzy. "We have to get to Julian!"

"Let's go," Eric said before he flew out the window. I started to go after him but something wasn't right.

I turned around to see my mom standing there looking healthy as a horse. "Mom," I called out looking at her through the Blackness of my eyes.

"Go," she mouthed. "I'm fine just go fight with your brothers."

"You're dead," I asked.

She nodded her head and I felt something rip from me. Anger ripped through me. I felt like my life was ending but I didn't want to let that feeling consume. I replace the sorrow with anger and rage.

"I'm going to find you," I said to her before I flew out the window.

It took all but two seconds to get to the island. Maybe it was just the anger from seeing my mom dead or the anger from seeing the pool of Julian's blood. Whatever carried me so fast blasted me right into Canicus.

"You son of a bitch," I screamed throwing orbs of fire and water at him. I picked up some rocks and aimed for his head. "Why did you kill my mom?"

Canicus laughed and turned into his Blackness form. "You're mom isn't dead. She is dying though. So let's end this quickly so you can die with her."

He flung me into a tree and I hit my head. Everything was blurry for a moment but I focused on him. I saw him trying to come at me again but I slid out the way before he could hit me.

I made an energy globe with spirit and pushed it at him with intense force that it knocked him almost twenty yards back. "I'm not going to die," I said forming glowing orbs of fire in my hands. "My mom's not going to die." I threw them at him and he fell to the ground. I turned into my Spirit form. "The only person dying today is you." I pushed another ball of energy toward him and he went up in flames.

I used the air around him and made a big tornado. I added earth, spirit and more fire to engulf him in it. He laughed it off.

"You silly bitch," he said through the wind. "This can't hurt me." He threw out his hands and everything went black.

It fell silent for a moment before everything exploded into a bright light. I felt a strong energy push me back into another tree making me hit my head again. I felt dizzier and touched my head to find blood.

"Evil always triumphs when I'm the evil one," he said towering over me. "You will lose, Roel. You should run away now."

I looked behind him to see Julian staring at me with plead and anger in his eyes. He was still bleeding and I could see the fight in him with trying to stay alive. He smiled weakly at me and I realized that I wasn't going to let him or anyone else die.

"You really don't get it do you," I said turning back into my Spirit form. I opened the ground under him and watched him fall a few feet. "Evil never wins," I said in an eerie voice. "The fairytales are always right. Good will triumph as long as I'm on their side. I pushed his Blackness side back inside of him and looked at the frail immortal that I was soon going to kill.

"You will never get the satisfaction of me letting you win," I said taking the air from his lungs and engulfing him in flames. I started to wrap my spirit around him. "As long as I live you will never win. I will make sure I am six feet under before you can have the chance to hurt anymore of my friends and family." I watched as the flames started to burn his body.

He couldn't scream because he didn't have the air in his lungs. I felt the Blackness from my eyes leak out of my body while I turned back into my human form. His body started to dissolve as I watched him disappear. When his body was fully gone everything lightened up again.

My eyes were back to normal and it felt so good to see again. The first thing I did was run to Julian. "Are you okay," I asked as I tried to retrieve the glass from his side.

"I'm bleeding to death but other than that I'm fine," he said barely in a whisper. When I pulled the glass from his side his body went rigid and then he went still.

"Julian," I said taking his face into my hands. "Hey, wake up," I yelled smacking him really hard.

"Ouch," he said squinting his eyes. "You definitely know how to kill a good dream, Roel." He touched his side. "I hope you can heal that," he said finally opening his eyes.

"And Julian is back," I laughed. I turned to see everyone not fighting anymore.

The demons, along with Elizabeth and Julia, looked confused as to why they were fighting their brothers and frenemies. Everyone looked battered and hurt but they all looked like they were going to live. The only person that was severely hurt was the one in my hands.

"Jared," I called out and Jared was beside me in the blink of an eye. "Help me fix his wound."

"You can do on your own," he said taking my hand and putting it on the bloody laceration on Julian's side. "Think of water cleaning his would and putting it back together. You may have an easier time doing it since you can control all five elements."

I concentrated on water and Julian's wound. I felt the element flow through my body and into his. His eyes lit up and I could tell he could feel it too. It felt relaxing and calming after the fight everyone was just in.

I looked up to find my mom standing over us. She was smiling and she looked even better than I saw her in my room. I looked back down to Julian and saw the wound had healed into a soft pink line across his stomach. I looked back up and my mom was gone.

"No," I said falling on my butt and backing away from everyone. "My mom's dead," I said rocking back and forth. "She's gone."

Chad came to my side and hugged me tightly. "I know," he said as he started crying beside me. "I feel her though. She's still here."

"But I can't see her anymore," I said grabbing his shirt and pulling him closer to me. "She's gone because I didn't get to her in time. It's all my fault."

No one commented on the thought and they let me cry and snot and sob on Chad's shoulder. When Julian had enough strength he crawled over to me and put his head on my chest. And we all sat there and cried. Not because I lost my mom. We cried because even though we won the battle Canicus really truly knew that he was going to win someway somehow. He took my mom and that was enough to hurt everyone's soul.

Epilogue

A month later

"So this is the last time I'll see you," I asked my mom as I sat down in my chair. "You won't be visiting me in my dreams anymore."

"You'll see me," she said lightly. "You can see souls. You freed me from Canicus's spell but I still have to stick around when you have a 'seeing souls' episode."

A tear escaped from my eyes. "It's not fair though. Why did he have to kill you?"

"It was inevitable," an all too familiar voice said from the shadows in the room. Canicus stepped out looking just the way he always did. His hair was a little longer and his eyes were more intense. "You look lovely, Roel."

I gave him a disgusted look. "Why are you here right now," I sneered. "You should be somewhere sulking about the battle you lost."

"Sorry if my behavior is not what you're looking for," he smiled. His smiled was like looking at the sun. It may be beautiful but you can't stare at it too long.

"What brings you to my head," I asked him crossing my arms and looking at the fire place.

"You, of course," he said. He summoned a chair next to me and sat in it. "You have sparked something in me that I find most fascinating."

I laughed sadistically. "I'm sorry, remind me to gag later."

"I'm serious, Roel," he said in an all too serious tone. He touched my hand and his skin was really warm.

I hastily slid my hand away from his. "You're crazy," I said. "You've been nothing but rude to me. Let's not even mention the fact that you tried to kill me the last time I saw you." I stood up and went to my mother. "You killed my mom."

"I can fix that," he said getting up from his chair. "I can give her another body."

I suppressed a laugh. "Yea, right," I laughed. "You're full of shit."

His face went from serious to amuse. "You're right I am full of shit. But you did fascinate me greatly." He blinked in front of me. "You fill me with passion and rage." He touched my face and I flinched. "I'll find you, princess. And when I find you I'll make you regret ever trying to kill me." He backed into the shadows and disappeared.

"I really hate that guy," I said sadistically. "I'm really gonna kill him one day."

"Honey," my mom said getting up and hugging me. "He's taken an interest in you that scares me. He said he likes you."

"I know mom," I said pulling away from her. "And I'm afraid that he's gonna take a little more interest in me than I want him to. Better yet, I think he already has."

"Wake up, honey," my mom said touching my forehead with her finger. "You have a play to attend."

"Wish me luck," I said and opened my eyes to the world where my mom no longer existed.